THE FURTHER ADVENTURES OF

JACK LIME

THE FURTHER ADVENTURES OF
JACK LIME

By James Leck

KCP FICTION

KCP Fiction is an imprint of Kids Can Press

Kids Can Press acknowledges the financial support of the Government of Ontario, through the Ontario Media Development Corporation's Ontario Book Initiative; the Ontario Arts Council; the Canada Council for the Arts; and the Government of Canada, through the CBF, for our publishing activity.

Published in Canada by
Kids Can Press Ltd.
25 Dockside Drive
Toronto, ON M5A 0B5

Published in the U.S. by
Kids Can Press Ltd.
2250 Military Road
Tonawanda, NY 14150

www.kidscanpress.com

Edited by Karen Li and Shana Hayes
Spot illustrations on cover and interior pages adapted from images © istockphoto/A-Digit/marlanu/johnwoodcock

This book is smyth sewn casebound.
Manufactured in Shenzen, China, in 11/2012 by C&C Offset Printing Co.

CM 13 0 9 8 7 6 5 4 3 2 1

Library and Archives Canada Cataloguing in Publication

Leck, James
The further adventures of Jack Lime / by James Leck.

ISBN 978-1-55453-740-2

I. Title.

PS8623.E397F87 2013 jC813'.6 C2012-904899-2

Kids Can Press is a Corus™ Entertainment company

For Zoe and Isaac, for keeping me fun and making me laugh.
For my parents and all their love. And for Heather,
who always keeps the faith and gives me the time.
It couldn't happen without you.

A NOTE FROM THE AUTHOR

What you are about to read are some of the more interesting cases that have crossed my desk. You see, I'm a detective, a private investigator, a gumshoe. What I do is fix problems for people who need their problems fixed. My name is Jack Lime, and these are my stories.

THE CASE OF THE MISSING QUARTERBACK

Tuesday, October 1, 12:04 p.m.
Iona High, The Cafeteria

If I had a sign that read Closed for Business, I would've had it stuck on my forehead in flashing neon letters. I was closed for business all right; I was closed big time. My nose was busted and covered in bandages; I had matching shiners and a head full of bad memories. It all had to do with a kid named Richie Renfrew, fifty bucks and a sticky-fingered goon named Malone. Sure, I solved the case, but I also got a knuckle sandwich from Malone and a night in the hospital listening to Old Doc Potter tell me to take a break from the private investigation game. Who am I to argue with a doctor? So, yeah, I was closed for business. All I wanted was a chance to enjoy my slice of pepperoni pizza in peace. That's when KC Stone walked into my life.

"Jack Lime," she said, sitting across from me. "Name's KC Stone. I heard you got that money back for Richard Renfrew, and I'd like to interview you for the newspaper. What d'you say?"

KC had thick red hair held back by a pair of sunglasses, freckles across her nose and wore a white T-shirt with the words "The Truth Hurts" fading away across the front.

"Sorry," I said. "I didn't do it for the publicity."

"It might help your detective agency," she said. "Attract some business."

"I don't need help with that," I said. "Now if you'll excuse me, I'd like to eat my pizza."

"It might give you a chance to stick it to Patrick Malone," she said. "By the looks of your nose, he stuck it to you."

"How do you know about that?"

"I'm a journalist, Jack. I have my ways."

"I'm not interested in being your Hero of the Week, sister, so you'll just have to find somebody else to interview."

KC smiled. "If you reconsider, let me know. But that's not the only reason I'm here. I have a favor to ask."

"Can you come back another time?" I asked, taking a bite of my pizza. It tasted like a cross between a piece of cardboard and an old shoe. "I'm trying to enjoy my lunch here."

"Give it a break, Lime," she said. "The pizza here tastes like a cross between a piece of cardboard and an old shoe. Plus, it's not me who needs your help. But if you're too busy to help a damsel in distress, then I'll pass her name on to somebody else."

I laughed. I couldn't help it. "A damsel in distress? That's rich. But sure, why not? Send her over. Maybe she's cooked up an elaborate double cross that involves yours truly getting duped, because those cases seem to be my specialty."

"Jeesh, Jack," she said, "I didn't realize you were so ... so ..."

"Hard-boiled? Cynical?"

"No," she said. "I didn't know you were so wordy. Do you always like to hear yourself talk so much?"

"Just bring her over," I growled, putting my pizza down and pushing it away.

KC came back with a girl who had skin the color of a Hershey's Kiss, curly black hair that hung down to her shoulders and dark brown eyes that reminded me of a warm cup of joe. She was wearing a black skirt with a matching black top and black sandals with sparkly doodads across the top.

"Close your mouth, Lime," KC snapped. "I wouldn't want you to swallow a fly. This is Betty Goodwin. She needs some help."

"Why don't you am-scray, Katie, so that Betty and I can talk off the record," I said. "Or does that rag you call a newspaper get kicks from publishing the troubles of innocent beauties ... I mean babes ... I mean girls."

"Are you sure this is a good idea?" Betty asked. "He doesn't look well."

"He's fine," KC said, pushing Betty into a chair. "He just pretends to be tough."

"Tough, dangerous, handsome; call me whatever you like, Betty. And as soon as your friend skedaddles, we can get down to business."

"Please stay," Betty said, grabbing KC's arm.

"Don't worry. He seems a little strange, but he won't bite. You won't bite, will you, Jack?"

"Not Betty," I said. KC rolled her eyes and exited stage right.

Betty glanced around the room before she started. "I feel kind of bad about telling you this," she said. "I mean ... I guess ... I guess I feel like it's kind of personal."

"Personal's what I do best, doll. Especially if it means getting my nose busted, so spit it out and I'll see what I can do."

"Okay," she said, taking a deep breath. "Well, my boyfriend is acting really strange. He'll run off at the weirdest times, and he won't tell me where he's going. Like last night, we were at my house, and we were just about to start a movie when he got a text message on his phone. I asked him who it was, but he wouldn't tell me. He just grabbed his things and left."

"Is that the first time he's done something like that?" I asked.

"No, he's been getting texts and then running off for about two weeks, maybe three."

"And he never tells you where he's going?"

"No, he just says he'll call later."

"Why don't you dump him?" I said. "A girl like you doesn't have to put up with a chump like that."

"But we're in love."

"Love? When you get a little older and wiser, you'll learn that love is just another word that starts with an *L*, like loser, lonely and liar. But, hey, if that's the way you feel, I'll see what I can do."

"I'm worried he's in some kind of trouble."

I shook my head. I had to. This poor, gullible girl was about to grow up — and fast. In my professional experience, when a guy disappears and doesn't tell his main squeeze where he's going, it usually means he's got another girlfriend on the side.

"You got a picture of Romeo?" I asked.

"Here," she said, handing over her phone. "But his name is Lance, not Romeo."

"I'll make sure I write that down somewhere," I said, taking a look at the photo on her cell. The guy staring back at me was blond, blue-eyed and had an easy smile that said he didn't have a care in the world. And why would he, with a girl like Betty on his arm?

"Meet me in the main foyer after school, and I'll tell you if I've managed to find anything out, capiche?"

"Ka-what?" she asked.

"Just meet me in the main foyer."

"'Kay," she said, and left.

I tossed my pizza in the garbage and went looking for Lance. I guess I was back in business.

Tuesday, October 1, 12:38 p.m.
Iona High, The Cafeteria

Lance wasn't hard to track down. Not only was he a couple of inches over six feet, but his carefully disheveled blond hair, square jaw and chiseled features made him look like a male model about to walk down the runway.

Plus, he was wearing one of those letterman jackets that advertised he was on the football team. I found him lounging around outside the gym with a bunch of his cronies, smiling at girls and looking smooth. I took up position down the hall and blended in by pretending to stare into space. My covert operation was going smoothly until Max Thorn stepped in front of me.

"Are you on a case, Lime?" he asked.

"Keep your voice down, Max," I said.

"I knew it. Who's our target?" he asked, glancing around the hall.

FYI — Max is a nutty kid who thinks he's always on some kind of top-secret mission. He also thinks he's my sidekick because he's helped me out on a couple of cases. I have to admit he can be handy to have around sometimes, especially if you're asleep and sinking to the bottom of the Iona River, but the last thing I needed right now was Max Thorn asking me a bunch of questions.

"He's not *our* target, Max. I work alone, remember?"

"Sure, Jack. So who are you watching?"

"The blond pretty boy in the football jacket."

"Lance Munroe?" he asked.

"That's the one. You know anything about him?"

"I don't have much intel on him, except that he arrived in Iona on July 8th, he lives at 10 Triton Court with his mom and dad and his golden retriever, Sam, and that he set every football record at his old high school."

"That's all you've got, Thorn?"

"Give me time, Sarge. Give me a little time. I can find out more."

"I guess I've been too busy solving cases for the down-and-out kids in this school to follow Lance Munroe around."

"Yeah, it looks like you've been sticking your nose in all the wrong places, Lime," he said with a chuckle. "What happened?"

"It's not important."

"I gotcha," he said with a wink, "it's top secret, but can you at least let me know what Lance did to get you on his trail? Was it kidnapping? Blackmail? Murder?"

"That's private information between me and my client, and I'm kind of busy here, Max, so why don't you make like a tree and leave."

"Sure," he said, "but I'd be careful, Sarge. Now that Lance is our star QB, he's a valuable commodity. He's got some important people watching his back. If you get too close, you might want to start watching your back, too."

"I'll keep that in mind," I said. "Now hit the bricks."

Max left and I got back to watching Lance do a whole lot of nothing for the rest of lunch break. I had a hunch that this was going to be a paint-by-numbers kind of case, and that was okay by me. A boring case was just what the doctor ordered.

Tuesday, October 1, 3:26 p.m.
Iona High, The Main Foyer

I tailed Lance between classes that afternoon, but he didn't do anything that was even remotely incriminating. When the final bell rang, I decided to skip tracking him down again and headed straight to the main foyer. Betty was standing in the far corner with KC, and she looked happy to see me. Unfortunately my investigation was a bust so far, and I had nothing to give her except for one of my dazzling smiles.

"Any news?" Betty asked.

"I've got nothing, nada, *niet.*"

"Knee-ette?" Betty asked.

"No news," I said.

"Is that good news?" KC asked.

"Could be, but why don't you give me a little more time, and I'll see what I can dig up."

"Please keep trying, Jack," Betty said, grabbing my hand. "I just know he's in some kind of trouble. Is there anything I can do to help?"

"Keep tabs on Lance," I said, handing her one of my business cards with my number on it. "Call me if anything unusual comes up."

"Sure," she said.

"And whatever you do, don't mention any of this to Lance."

"'Kay."

"Anything I can do, Lime?" KC asked.

"Just make sure none of this ends up in your gossip rag. Remember, I don't want to be made into some kind of hero."

"I think I can handle that," she said, and we all went our separate ways.

Thursday, October 3, 8:06 p.m.
A street with no name, Grandma's House

For the next two days, I watched Lance hang out with his buddies, make eyes at Betty and practice football. I was starting to think this was all in Betty's head. She was beautiful, sure, but that didn't mean she couldn't be a little loony, too. I was just getting used to working on a case going nowhere when Betty called Thursday night.

"He left again," she said.

"What happened?"

"We were working on math homework together and he got a text. He couldn't even read it in front of me, Jack. He got up and read it in the kitchen, and then he grabbed his things and left."

"Where did he say he was going?"

"He wouldn't tell me. He just said he'd see me tomorrow and left," she said, sniffling. "Do you think it's another girl?"

"That's crazy talk, Betty," I said, trying hard to sound like I was telling the truth. "How long has he been gone?"

"About two minutes."

"Did you see which way he went?"

"No."

"That's too bad," I said. "He could be anywhere by now. The next time he disappears like that, I need you to see which way he's going. Then I might have a chance to latch on to his trail. You got that?"

"'Kay," she said. Now she was crying.

"But if you really want to know what he's been up to, I'll need to take a look at some of those text messages. Is his phone locked down with a password?"

"Uh-huh," she said through sniffles.

"Do you know what it is?"

"It's 0-3-1-4," she said. "That's my birthday, March 14th." And that's when the waterworks really started.

"Listen to me, Betty," I said. "I promise to find out what he's been up to. Do you hear me?"

"Thanks, Jack," she said.

"I'll let you know tomorrow."

"'Kay," she said, and hung up.

I didn't think I'd find much on Lance's phone, but it was still worth looking into. Besides, if he was fool enough to be running out on a girl like Betty, he was fool enough to slip up sooner or later, and when he did, I'd be waiting.

Friday, October 4, 3:15 p.m.
Iona High, Mr. Kurtz's Class

Cell phones aren't that easy to steal, and Lance was extra careful with his. He didn't leave it lying on any tables, and he had a habit of checking his pockets every thirty seconds to make sure it was still there. I was getting worried that I might miss my chance, so I decided to try an old pickpocketing technique known as the bump and run. After lunch, I tailed Lance to his locker and casually strolled toward him with my nose stuck in my history book. Just as he closed the locker door, I ran into him. The plan was to bounce off him, drop the textbook and grab his cell when he was bending over to pick the book up. Unfortunately Lance is built like a brick wall, and my bounce was more like a flying leap into the lockers that ended with me lying spread-eagled on the ground.

"Watch it," he said, looking down at me. I don't think he even noticed my textbook lying against the wall on the other side of the hallway as he walked away.

I decided to try to concoct a different plan to nab his phone during last class, but Mr. Kurtz, my English teacher, sprang a test on us out of the blue. When I complained, he pointed at the homework board and claimed that he'd been warning the class about the test for two weeks. I pointed out that he could've written that on the board at any time, since he had easy access to the classroom. Plus, he had motive, which was obviously to make us suffer. Everyone in class was behind me, and I would've won the argument, except Kurtz conveniently avoided the issue by moving me and my desk into the hall.

"You have one hour to finish, Mr. Lime," he said, slapping the test on my desk. "So you better stop wagging your tongue and start moving your pen."

I was just writing a witty answer to the last question when the end-of-day announcements came over the PA. Besides the usual gobbledygook about art contests and student fees, there was a reminder to come out and support the boys' football team. Apparently they had an important game against Eastern High that afternoon.

I dotted the last *t* and crossed the last *i*, handed in my test and headed for the football field. I might finally get a chance to look at those texts, after all.

Friday, October 4, 4:27 p.m.
Iona High, The Football Field

It was a sunny fall afternoon, the perfect kind of day to watch a football game. The place was swarming with kids jostling for good seats and gossiping about the average, ordinary things that go on in their average, ordinary lives. I spotted Betty in the front row, looking anxious. KC was off to the side with a pen and a notepad, and I was sitting in the top row of the bleachers taking it all in. Lance led the Iona High Warriors onto the field, but when the whistle blew, he didn't look like much of a star to me. Sure, he could fire a ball down the field like it'd been shot out of a cannon, and he could run faster than a cheetah with his tail on fire, but he fumbled the ball once and threw two interceptions, all in the first quarter. By the time the second quarter started, Iona was down by fourteen and the crowd was getting restless. That's when I decided to make my move.

I casually strolled out of the stands, wandered over to the school and slipped into the side door of the gymnasium. The boys' change room was connected to the bathroom, giving me a perfectly plausible alibi for snooping around. Luckily the place was empty, and finding Lance's jacket was a cinch, since his name was stitched on the sleeve.

Sure enough, I found his cell in his pocket, and I was about to start typing in his password when Mr. Leoni, the school custodian, burst in.

"What are you doing in here, kid? There's a porta-potty outside for the fans."

"I have really bad toilets," I said, jamming the phone in my pocket, "so I need to use the cramp, and fast." Before he could say anything, I bolted into one of the bathroom stalls.

"Just make sure you flush when you're done," he hollered, and stomped out.

I pulled out the phone and typed in 0-3-1-4. Lance might've been paranoid about his phone, but he wasn't paranoid enough to delete his call history from yesterday. He'd gotten 188 text messages, but only one had been sent right around the time that he'd run off on Betty. That one came in at 8:03, and it was sent from someone called Red. According to the contact info, Red's number was 555-3333. I opened the message. This is all it said:

R side P. Now.

In the movies, detectives always seem to figure out secret messages lickety-split, but that can be hard to do when you're standing in a bathroom stall and you know that Mr. Leoni is lurking around waiting for you to finish with your business. Plus, I didn't have long to consider the possibilities because a couple of eggs came in and started yakking about the game. I peeked through the gap next to the stall door and spotted a tall drink of water with brown hair and bad acne. He was standing beside a short, plump kid sporting a crew cut.

"Eastern's going to win for sure," Tall and Pimply said.

"If Lance is off, we don't have a chance," Crew Cut added.

"So what can I put you guys down for?" a familiar voice asked. I leaned a little to my left and saw Mike the Bookie holding a pencil and notepad.

For those of you who haven't been following my career as closely as you should, Mike the Bookie is a shifty grifter who was the numbers man for a criminal mastermind named Tobias Poe. Tobias worked a scam on yours truly that ended with me losing my laptop, my cell and a significant chunk of change. Tobias graduated last year and moved on to bigger and nastier places, but Mike was still prowling around Iona High with his little black book, taking money from every dumb mug that came his way.

"Put me down for fifty that Eastern wins," Tall and Pimply said.

"Me too," Crew Cut added.

Mike scratched down the bets in his notebook, then headed for the door. That's when Leoni stormed back in, flexing the muscles in his handlebar mustache.

"How many times do I got to tell you kids there's a toilet outside for the fans!"

They all nodded and tried to scurry out, but Leoni stepped in front of the door.

"Don't forget your friend," he said pointing in my direction.

That was my cue to leave. I flushed the toilet, strolled out and acted casual. Mike's jaw hit the floor and the two rubes stared at me like they'd seen a ghost.

"I found this," I said, handing Lance's phone over to Leoni. "You should tell the owner to be more careful. There are a lot of thieves roaming around this school who have very sticky fingers, right, Mike?"

"I don't know what you're talking about," he said.

"Sure he does," I said, looking from one dumb mug to the other. "Sure he does."

"You don't know squat about football," Tall and Pimply said, smirking.

"Yeah," his friend chirped in, "stick to finding bicycles, Lime."

I was going to remind them that a rube and his money are soon parted when Leoni put an end to our little give and take.

"Get outta here!" he yelled, curling his hands into fists. "The lot of ya!"

He didn't have to ask twice. Mike and the two knuckleheads bolted outside and went one way and I went the other. I got back to my seat just in time to watch Lance fumble the ball one more time. Lucky for Lance the ref blew the whistle for halftime before Eastern could put any more points on the board. The teams jogged off the field, and the average, ordinary kids in the stands went back to talking about their average, ordinary lives. Me, I got to thinking about calling Lance's mystery friend, Red. But, like I said before, thanks to Tobias Poe I don't have a cell anymore, so that call would have to wait until later. For now I'd have to be content with the Iona High marching band's halftime show.

Friday, October 4, 5:14 p.m.
Iona High, The Football Field

Lance started the second half by throwing another interception. Coach Shultz pulled him aside and yelled up one side of him and down the other. The two rubes from the bathroom weren't too upset with Lance's terrible performance, though. They were sitting a few rows down from me and low-fiving every time Eastern High got a little closer to the Warriors' end zone. They got downright giddy when Eastern kicked a field goal at the end of the third quarter and went up by twenty points. When the fourth quarter started, people began to trickle out of the stands. Oddly, that's when Bucky King decided to show up.

FYI — Bucky King is a rather large and nasty galoot who runs a gang of hoodlums and tough guys known as the Riverside Boys. He's the current kingpin of the criminal underworld at Iona High and has his gigantic, hairy fingers in everything from extortion to the sale of stolen goods.

Bucky's usually not the type of guy to stand around watching a football game, so when he took up position behind the fence on the far side of the field I got interested. I got even more interested when Mike the Bookie slithered up beside him. Mike whispered a few things in Bucky's ear and then exited stage right. Bucky lit up a cigarette, puffed on it for a minute and then flicked it on the ground and left. Besides being responsible for a serious fire hazard, Bucky, I had a hunch, was up to no good. Something fishy was going on here, but I didn't have much time to think about it because that's when the crowd went wild. Lance Munroe had just thrown a seventy-five-yard pass downfield for a touchdown.

In the future, when people talk about great athletic accomplishments at Iona High, the last quarter of that game is sure to come up. Not only did Lance play offense, he played defense, too. He ran around the field like a crazy squirrel in a nut factory. He intercepted passes, he ran through tackles, he threw two touchdowns and ran one in with three opposing players hanging off his back. When the final whistle blew and the fat lady sang, the Warriors were up by one and Lance was the toast of the town.

Most of the fans paraded out of the stands laughing and cheering, but there were a few who looked more than a little disappointed. Heck, they looked downright angry, and I had a sneaking suspicion they'd all just lost a bunch of dough betting that Eastern High was a sure thing to win. They were probably wondering why Lance waited until the last minute to play like a superhero. I was beginning to wonder that myself. I was beginning to wonder about a lot of things, and I figured the easiest way to get some of the answers was to catch up with Lance "The Miracle Man" Munroe.

Friday, October 4, 6:17 p.m.
17 Sea of Tranquility Lane, The Goodwin Place

A little after six, Lance came out the school's main doors with Betty and a crowd of kids who were still hooting about his incredible performance. They took off in a whirlwind of excitement, but gradually the groupies trailed away in different directions. By the time we arrived at a cozy white house with a picket fence around the front, it was just the two of them. The name on the mailbox said "The Goodwins," and I watched the lovebirds go inside. Then I found a comfortable tree to lean against across the street and settled down to do some thinking. Unfortunately any thinking I was about to do was rudely interrupted when KC Stone stepped up beside me.

"What are you doing here, Lime?"

"KC," I said, turning around. "Nice of you to drop by. You always make my other problems seem insignificant."

"A detective of your stature must have serious problems — like hangnails and out-of-control nose hairs."

"Are you here to groom me or just to bother me?"

"Actually I'm here to have dinner and interview Lance. He had an incredible game this afternoon."

"Yeah," I said, "a very convenient last-minute comeback."

"Care to expand on that, Lime?"

"I don't think I can, not yet, but something doesn't smell right around here, and I'm planning on finding out what's baking in the oven."

"I'm not sure what that means, but try to keep your head screwed on straight," she said. "I wouldn't want you to end up looking like a fool."

"I'm not going to make you any promises."

"That's probably a good decision, Jack. Is there anything I can do to help?"

"Call me if Lance does anything suspicious," I said, handing her one of my cards.

"Like winning a football game?"

"Exactly," I said.

KC rolled her eyes and headed across the street.

I decided I didn't want to lean against a tree for the rest of the night while Lance sat inside and ate a warm meal. Plus, I usually met my grandma for supper at The Diner on Friday nights, and I had about five minutes to get there before she thought I'd stood her up. On top of all that, I was willing to bet dollars to doughnuts that Lance wasn't going anywhere tonight, not after a game like that and not when he had Betty and KC gushing all over him.

Friday, October 4, 6:32 p.m.
29A Main Street, The Diner

I walked through the door at The Diner just as Moses was giving Grandma her dinner. I apologized for being tardy, ordered a bacon-and-cheese burger with fries on the side and a root beer float, and then strolled over to the pay phone in the back. I dialed 555-3333 and waited to see who would pick up.

The phone rang five times before an automated recording cut in and said, "Leave a message." There was a beep. I hung up and went back to our booth. The number might be a dead end for now, but I had plenty of time to call again.

"Your nose is looking better," Moses said, sliding my root beer float in front of me.

"Thanks," I said, and was just about to take my first sip when the pay phone started to ring.

I bolted out of the booth and picked it up on the third ring.

"Hello," I said.

"How did you get this number?" the person on the other end asked. The voice sounded robotic, as if it was being electronically altered.

"What do you mean, how'd I get this number?" I said, playing a hunch. "This is Lance. What's up?"

"You're not Lance."

"What do you mean? I ought to know who I am, pal. This is Lance Munroe. Now you better tell me who you are before I come over there and twist you into a human pretzel."

Unfortunately the yahoo on the other end wasn't buying what I was selling and hung up.

"What was that about, Jack?" Grandma asked, as I slid back into the booth. "I thought we agreed you were taking a break from being a detective."

"It's an open-and-shut case," I said. "There's nothing to it."

"Nothing's simple," Grandma said.

"You might be right."

"Of course I'm right," she said, grabbing some of my fries, "and I don't want to deal with any more visits to the hospital. Do we understand each other?"

"Sure, no more visits to the hospital," I said, and took a long drink from my float.

Friday, October 4, 7:59 p.m.
Grandma's House, The Kitchen

I scarfed down my burger, stuffed my face with fries, gulped down my float and finished the whole thing off with an enormous piece of lemon meringue pie. Grandma stuck around at The Diner to listen to the end of the ball game, so I rolled home on my own. As I stepped onto the front porch, the kitchen phone started to ring and I rushed inside.

"Hello," I gasped.

"Jack," a voice said, in no more than a whisper, "I need your help."

"Betty?"

"Lance got another one of those texts. He rushed out, but I followed him this time, just like you said."

"Betty, I told you to find out which way he went, not to follow him. Where are you?"

"I'm in Riverside Park. At the big field with the tennis courts. Please, you've got to come down here."

"I'll be there faster than you can say game, set and match."

I got my bike and headed for Riverside Park. I'd found the bike over the summer, sitting in the back corner of the garage, covered in dust. It had belonged to my dad and needed a little work, so I spent July mowing lawns and used the money to spruce it up. Now it was as good as new and a handy way for me to get places quick, fast, in a hurry.

I made it to the park in no time flat and parked my bike under a tree. Then I crept along the path until I had a clear view of the tennis courts, which were on the far side of the field and illuminated by four towering outdoor lights. I was expecting to see Lance making out with a girl, but instead there was a heated game of dodgeball under way. A cluster of about a dozen yahoos was standing outside the fence that surrounded the courts, watching the action. I'd just taken a few steps toward the field when a dark figure sprang out of the shadows and grabbed my wrist.

I yanked my hand free and lunged. We toppled backward into the trees, rolled around and I came out on top. I was about to teach this mooyuk a lesson in manners when my condition kicked in and everything went black.

FYI — Thanks to my condition, I don't get to choose when I go to sleep. Old Doc Potter calls it narcolepsy; I call it a curse because it tends to kick in at the worst times. Like right now I'm in the middle of defending myself from an unknown assailant when my body decides it's time for a quick visit to Never-Never Land.

I dreamed I was in a room with blood-red carpets and walls to match. KC Stone was standing in front of me. Her hair was down, hanging in long red waves over her shoulders. She was wearing a big, poufy white dress that made it look like she was on her way to the prom.

"The fix is in, Jack."

"What do you mean?" I said.

"It's all a setup."

"I don't believe you," I said.

"The wheels are already in motion," she said.

"What do you mean?"

"Wake up and smell the roses, Jack."

"I don't understand," I said, but now she was sinking into the carpet. She was already up to her knees, and her dress was soaking up the red like a paper towel.

"I don't understand," I said, trying to pull her out.

"I know," she said. "Now wake up!"

I tried to hold on to her hand but I was too weak and she slipped away, sinking down into the carpet, like it had changed into quicksand.

"Wake up," a voice said. It sounded far away.

"I don't understand," I mumbled.

"Wake up, Jack," the voice said again, but now it was Betty's voice. I opened my eyes to see her kneeling beside me.

"Jack, are you okay?"

"I think so," I said, sitting up. Betty was wearing a black leather jacket, black jeans and a black wool hat. Long story short, she looked like a million bucks.

"What happened?" I asked. "Where did you come from?"

"I was waiting for you in the trees," she said. "I grabbed your hand when you walked by, but you attacked me. I guess you must've hit your head or something."

"Sorry about that," I said. "I can get as jittery as a chipmunk at a bloodhound convention when I'm on a case."

"A bloodhound convention?" she said, looking confused.

"Forget about it," I said, standing up. "What we need to focus on now is why Lance came down here tonight."

"I just want to know why he's running away from me," she said.

"You might not like what we find out."

She nodded and we crept to the other side of the field, staying in the trees. I found a good vantage point behind a couple of evergreens about twenty feet from the action. Lance was playing on a team with two big oafs who could barely lumber their way around the court. One was Derek Sanders, a longtime member of the Riverside Boys, who most people call Heavy because he weighs about as much as a full-grown grizzly bear. The other one was Patrick Malone, the same bruno who busted my nose last Friday. The other team was made up of three pip-squeaks who looked like they'd just graduated from Iona Elementary. They were buzzing around the court like wasps in fast-forward, firing balls left, right and center. It didn't take them long to blast Heavy and Malone out of the game. Lance, however, was a whole lot quicker and harder to hit. He jumped over, ducked under and bent around everything the pip-squeaks sent his way. He evened things up when he sent two balls hurtling across the court like a couple of heat-seeking missiles and two of the pip-squeaks went down like sacks of wet cement. Now it was Lance "The Football Star" Munroe vs. a kid who might've weighed in at ninety pounds soaking wet. That's when the gawkers on the sidelines started waving their dough in the air and crowding around two crooks I knew all too well — Mike the Bookie and Bucky King.

Mike was taking cash and scribbling down names in his little black book while Bucky stood around looking tough and making sure people waited their turn.

"What's going on?" Betty whispered, crouching close to me. I could smell the faint scent of watermelon bubblegum on her breath and I forgot all about the case, and being a detective, and my busted schnoz. I forgot about Bucky King and Mike the Bookie, but most of all I forgot about Lance Munroe. I forgot about everything except for Betty and the smell of watermelon bubblegum, and for a second there, dear reader, all my troubles were gone, kaput, vanished.

"Jack, are you okay?" Betty asked, breaking the spell.

"Yeah," I mumbled, and the world came flooding back into focus.

"What's going on?" she asked again.

"After hours of fun for thugs and rubes," I said, shaking my head to clear it out, "dodgeball was banned by Principal Snit last year when a bunch of kids went home with mysterious bruises, busted lips and empty wallets. Parents started asking questions and found out their not-so-innocent offspring were losing their allowance betting on dodgeball games. The whole thing was organized by Bucky King and his gang of thugs. I hate to tell you this, Betty, but it looks like Lance is running out on you because he's connected to the Riverside Boys."

"I can't believe that, Jack," Betty mumbled. "He'd never be part of a gang."

Before I could say anything else, Bucky told the crowd to back off. Apparently the time for betting was done and everyone's attention turned back to the court. Lance was firing laser-beam shots at the Last of the Pip-squeaks, and the crowd oohed and aahed every time the little guy managed to get out of the way. It looked like it was only a matter of time before Lance finished him off when the pip-squeak heaved a ball in Lance's direction. Lance was sidestepping out of the way when he tripped and fell. The ball bounced once and then glanced off his shoulder. Team Pip-squeak ran onto the court and gave one another high-fives while the gawkers on the outside of the fence stood around with their jaws open.

"The fix is in," I mumbled.

"What?" Betty asked.

I was about to explain that Lance had obviously lost the game on purpose when we were rudely interrupted.

"Sorry to break up your little snuggle session," a deep voice said from behind us, "but this is a private party."

Betty grabbed my arm and screamed. I spun around with my dukes up, ready for a shakedown. That's when Ronny Kutcher stepped out of the shadows. Ronny is a doughy little kid I had as a client not that long ago. He was the type of guy who couldn't punch his way out of a paper bag, so I relaxed a little.

"Ronny, what's the big idea —" I started, but he cut me off.

"They're down here, boss!"

I grabbed Betty's hand and tried to clear out of there, but we only managed to cover a few feet before Bucky stepped in front of us, a cigarette dangling from his mouth. Heavy and Malone came lumbering up behind him like two trained monkeys.

"What's the rush, Lime?" Bucky asked.

"No rush," I said. "It's just that the stink of sleaze around here was starting to make me sick."

Bucky frowned, strolled over to Ronny and gave him a pat on the back. "Ronny's our lookout. He called me as soon as you arrived."

"Great job, Ronny," I said, "but you should probably run along. A kid your size needs his rest."

Ronny got all hot under the collar and tried to make a run at me, but Bucky grabbed his shirt and held him back.

"What are you doing here?" Bucky asked.

"Oh, I don't know," I said, "just watching you run a crooked gambling racket."

"Gambling?" Bucky said with a smile. "I didn't see any gambling? Did you see any gambling, Lance?"

I spun around again. Lance, Mike the Bookie and the rest of the slack jaws from the audience were standing behind us.

"I didn't see any gambling," Lance said.

"What's going on?" Betty cried, running to Lance. "Jack says you're involved with a gang?"

"He's got it all wrong, Betty," Lance said, pulling her away.

"Don't listen to him, Betty!" I said. "He's mixed up in this dirty mess tighter than a guinea pig at a boa constrictor party!"

"Mind your own business, Lime," Lance growled.

I tried to go after her, but Bucky must've let Ronny go because the little guy was suddenly pummeling me with his tiny fists. It was like having a Chihuahua bite at your heels, and by the time I pushed him away, Betty was gone.

"You should get a leash for your puppy," I said to Bucky. "Or he might get into some real trouble one of these days."

"You're the only one who's going to get into trouble around here, Lime," Ronny yapped. "You and your antique bike."

"Gee, I'd love to stick around and chat about bicycles, Ronny. I know it's one of your favorite topics, but I have to talk to a girl about her no-good dirty boyfriend."

"You're not going to talk to anyone," Bucky said, grabbing my wrist.

"What's it going to be this time, Bucky? Are you going to toss me in the river again?"

"Nah, I think we've done enough damage for one night. Don't you, Ronny?" he said with a sneer.

"Sure," Ronny said, chuckling, "we've done plenty of damage."

"Plus," Bucky added, handing me over to Heavy and Malone, "we've still got dodgeball to play. Have a good walk home, Limey."

Bucky and his lemmings headed back to the tennis courts while Heavy and Malone carried me back to the far side of the field and dumped me in the grass.

"You think I ought to bust his nose again, Heavy?" Malone asked, cracking his knuckles.

"Nah, he's too ugly already."

"Looks like it's your lucky day, Lime," Malone said, standing over me. "And if you know what's good for you, don't come crawling back."

"I know what's good for me, all right," I called, as they started back across the field. "And it has nothing to do with watching two washed-up scumbags pretending to play dodgeball!"

They ignored me and I staggered into the trees. I found my bike and suddenly understood what Bucky and Ronny had been chuckling about. Damage had been done, serious damage. My bike looked like it'd been attacked by a man-eating tiger; the seat was ripped, the tires were slashed, the spokes were bent and broken, the handlebar was turned around and the chain was off. It was a dirty move. It was rotten, despicable, underhanded and crooked. It was everything that was wrong with this little town, and I was tired of it. I was tired of bullies and goons pushing kids around. I was tired of golden boys like Lance Munroe pretending to be squeaky clean. Most of all I was tired of getting my nose busted and my bicycle broken, all in the name of solving a case. Well, this wasn't just about solving a case anymore. This was personal, and it was time for some payback.

Saturday, October 5, 12:12 p.m.
Main Street, The Diner

I tossed and turned all night, trying to think up a few different ways to get Bucky to pay for my broken bicycle, but there were no easy answers when it came to Bucky King. Sure, I could put the screws to Ronny Kutcher and get him to cough up the cash, but I didn't feel much like pushing around a little kid like him, even if he was working with the Riverside Boys. Nothing clever was coming to mind, so by noon on Saturday I decided to head to The Diner and drown my sorrows in a few dozen root beer floats.

I threw back my first one, grabbed a napkin and jotted down everything I knew about the case so far.

1. Lance was getting text messages from someone named Red at 555-3333.
2. Thanks to his last-minute comeback against Eastern High, more than a few kids had lost a tidy chunk of change to Bucky and Mike the Bookie.
3. Lance got a text last night and ran out on Betty to go play dodgeball in Riverside Park.
4. Lance was clearly working with the Riverside Boys to rig dodgeball games.
5. Somebody, probably Ronny Kutcher, had sunk his dirty claws into my innocent bike and ripped it to shreds.

I'd just finished making my list when KC Stone strolled in.

"How did you find me?" I asked.

"I'm a journalist, Jack. I have my ways."

"Well, take a hike," I said. "I'm busy."

"Right, you're obviously trying to come up with some kind of crazy scheme," she said, sliding into the booth across from me, "but Betty asked me to pass along a message. She's taking you off the case."

"Technically speaking, Stone, I'm not on that case anymore."

"What do you mean?"

"Betty hired me to find out where Lance was going after he got those text messages. I showed her last night."

"You mean that stuff about being in a gang?"

"That's right. I thought Lance was just busy making sweet with a girl on the side, but it turns out he's helping Bucky King rig underground dodgeball games. I'm also pretty sure he's a key part in fixing it so football games at this school start out one way and end another."

"Those are some pretty wild accusations, Jack. Do you have any proof?"

"I'll get some," I said. "You should sharpen your pencils and buy a few extra notepads, Stone, because this is going to be a doozy of a story when the poop hits the fan."

"Good luck with that, Jack," she said, sliding out of the booth. "By the way, Lance told Betty he was just helping out a few friends last night, and he's kind of angry about you saying he's in a gang. I'd stay away from him for a few years if I were you."

"Thanks for the tip, doll."

"No problem," she said. "And, Jack, if you call me doll again, you're going to have more than Lance to worry about."

KC walked out before I had a chance to hit her with a snappy comeback, but as much as I hated to admit it, she was right about Lance. If he saw me snooping around, he'd punch first and ask questions later. Then where would I be? Probably back in the hospital listening to Old Doc Potter tell me how I should take a break from the detective game, which is exactly what I was trying to do before KC Stone dragged me into this mess. Now all I wanted was to scrape up enough money to fix my bike, but even doing that was complicated. Ronny and Lance were out of the question, and only a fool would go after Bucky, so who was left? I stared into my float. The last glob of vanilla ice cream was clinging to the side of the mug. I pushed it down with my spoon, stirred it around and looked over my notes again. That phone number, 555-3333, was staring back at me. Somebody was on the other end of that number. Somebody who was connected to Bucky's operation. Somebody who knew times and places. Somebody with information about the betting that was going on in this town. As far as I knew, there was only one person at Iona High who fit that bill perfectly, and I was pretty sure I knew how to get him to help out with this investigation, whether he wanted to or not. But to do that, I needed to come up with a plan. And to do that, I needed another root beer float.

Sunday, October 6, 2:21 p.m.
76 Triton Court, The Putz Residence

I spent the rest of the weekend working out my plan. First I made a call to an old client named Gregory Pepperton, who still owed me a favor. Then I tracked down Tall and Pimply, the rube from the bathroom who'd lost a wad of dough betting against Lance and the Warriors. His actual name is Stanley Putz, and I decided to pay him a visit on Sunday afternoon. His mom answered the door and invited me in for some milk and cookies. I was just sitting down at the kitchen table when Stanley walked in.

"What do you want, Lime?" he asked.

"Stanley," his mother snapped, "that's no way to talk to a guest."

"It's all right, ma'am," I said. "Stanley's probably still upset about something I said on Friday. I wanted to come over and apologize."

"Well, then," she said, wiping her hands on her apron, "I'll just let you two boys work it out. I'll be in the den if you need anything, Stanley."

"What are you doing here?" he asked, snatching the cookie off my plate and taking a big bite.

"Lance's comeback the other day was something else, wasn't it?"

"Sure," he said, "but what's it to you?"

"I'll tell you what it is to me, friend. I think it's all too convenient. It's too convenient for Mike, and it's too convenient for Lance Munroe. The only person it's not convenient for is you and your short friend."

"Ollie?"

"What if I told you I know a surefire way for you and Ollie to get your money back."

"I'd say you were nuts, Lime."

"Hear me out, and if you still think I'm loony tunes at the end of my speech, then I'll leave you and your cookies alone forevermore. What do you say?"

"This better be good," he said, sitting down.

"It's better than good," I said, and explained my plan.

Monday, October 7, 12:10 p.m.
Iona High, The Cafeteria

Stanley Putz didn't think my plan was nuts. In fact, he liked it enough that he convinced his friend Ollie to help us out. I called Pepperton on Sunday night to confirm that the operation was a go, and by lunch on Monday, the trap was set.

At precisely ten minutes after twelve, I watched Stan and Ollie walk into the cafeteria from my position in a nearby stairwell. Five minutes later they came out with Mike the Bookie. Unfortunately Heavy stomped out behind them. I'd been afraid that my visit to the dodgeball game the other night might've spooked him. I figured he might have a little extra protection today, so I'd arranged for a diversion. That's where Gregory Pepperton fit into this plan.

Mike and the rubes filed into the boys' bathroom while Heavy guarded the door and looked mean.

Pepperton was standing at the end of the hall. I gave him a nod, and he came my way carrying four large boxes.

"What you got there?" Heavy asked as Pepperton walked by.

"Doughnuts," Pepperton said with a smile. "I'm giving them away in the cafeteria!"

"I have a better idea, Poindexter," Heavy said, stepping forward. "Why don't you give them to me and save yourself a lot of trouble."

"But ... I'm supposed to ..." Pepperton stammered, then he decided it'd be a whole lot easier to just make a break for the cafeteria. Heavy clomped after him while I darted across the hall and slipped into the boys' bathroom. The two rubes were about to place their bets when I arrived.

"Are you sure you want to bet that much?" Mike asked. "Do you guys even have that much money?"

"We're good for it," Stanley said, flashing a thick roll of banknotes.

Mike took out his little black book and scribbled down the bets.

"You know," I said, strolling toward Mike, "I wouldn't mind betting a few bones on the Warriors."

"Get lost, Lime!" Mike barked.

"What? Can't I bet on the game, too?"

"Sanders! Get in here!" Mike hollered.

"Heavy is busy chasing doughnuts," I said. "So you may as well put a lid on it."

Mike tried to tuck his notebook into his pocket, but Stanley snatched it away and handed it over.

"What's the deal!" Mike yelled.

"This little black book of yours has a lot of incriminating evidence in it," I said, flipping through the pages. "There are a lot of names with a lot of numbers, which means there are going to be a lot of kids in big trouble when I hand this over to Principal Snit."

"You wouldn't," Mike said.

"You bet I would, buster," I said. "I'd be happy to nail a small-time flimflam artist like you, Mike. And when Snit gets a load of this book, he's going to expel you faster than you can say GED."

"You're bluffing," Mike said.

"No, I'm not," I said. "But there might be a way for you to squirm out of this mess."

"You're both going to be in a heap of trouble when I walk out of here," Mike said, staring down the two rubes.

I heard one of them gulp and knew I needed to finish this fast.

"You're not going to touch a single hair on their sweet little heads, Mikey. If you do, I'm going straight to Snit, and you're going to be the fall guy for this nasty gambling operation. But you can end it all right here. All you have to do is three very simple things. First, you give these two unlucky saps their fifty bucks back. Second, you pay me one hundred and twenty-five bones. That's what it's going to cost to fix my bike. And last but not least, you're going to send Lance Munroe a text tonight at eight o'clock. Just like the messages you've been sending him all along."

"I don't know what you're talking about, Lime," Mike said.

"Spare me your lies, Mike," I said, and handed him one of my business cards. "I wrote what you're going to say on the back. My number's on the other side. You're going to call me when it's done. If Lance shows up tonight, none the wiser, then I'll give you back this book tomorrow at four o'clock. Meet me at The Diner on Main Street and bring the money for my bike. You got all that?"

"Even if I do all this, Lime, you won't give me back that book."

"Sure I will," I said. "You come through on your end and I'll give it back, no funny business."

"You'll just make a copy of it."

"No copies," I said.

Mike gritted his teeth.

"That or I go to Snit, and I'm sure Bucky won't be happy about all this. He'll have to blame somebody, right? My money's on you, Mike."

"Fine," Mike barked. He reached into his pocket, pulled out a wad of cash and tossed fifty bucks at each of the rubes. They grabbed their money off the floor and ran out. I eased my way back toward the door.

"Remember," I said, "you do your part and I'll do mine."

"You better," he growled, and I left him standing in the bathroom.

I considered making a beeline for the poetry section at the back of the library. I figured that was the perfect spot to lie low while I waited to see what Mike would do next. But before I went into hiding, I needed to find Gregory Pepperton and make sure he'd survived his run-in with Heavy. The last thing I needed right now was a new client.

Monday, October 7, 1:22 p.m.
Iona High, History Class

I had history after lunch and my teacher, Mr. Boardem, spent most of the class showing us pictures of his trip to Italy over the summer. I took the opportunity to thumb through Mike's gambling ledger. There were no surprises; it was filled with names, dates and amounts. I recognized most of the names, but there was one that kept coming up again and again — Lance Munroe. That was surprising, considering I had him pegged for an inside man in this betting operation. Why would Lance be losing money hand over fist if he was in on everything? I was considering the implications of this new information when Mr. Boardem interrupted my train of thought.

"Mr. Lime," he said, "could you please identify the building that I'm standing in front of in this photograph?"

"Ah," I mumbled, "is it Buckingham Palace?"

"Buckingham Palace is in London, Mr. Lime! This is in Rome. It is the Coliseum! Now please put away your little black book and pay attention. Who knows, you might learn something."

I was going to learn something, all right. Betty was going to learn something, and Lance was going to learn something, too. We were all going to learn something; it's just that some of us weren't going to like it. Nope, some of us weren't going to like it, not one little bit.

I watch your every move
—A

~~Monday,~~ October 7, 3:24 p.m.
Iona High, The Main Foyer

I was hiding behind a large plastic fern in the main foyer when KC Stone walked by at the end of the day.

"Psst!" I said.

She looked around.

"Psst!"

"Jack," she asked, peeking through the fern, "what are you doing back there?"

"Hiding."

"Really," she said, "I never would've guessed."

"Enough with the chitchat, Stone. I need you to do me a favor."

"I don't know. I usually don't do favors for boys who hide behind ferns."

"Hardee-har-har," I said. "You got me into this case with Betty and Lance, so now I need you to help me finish it."

"I thought you weren't on that case anymore?"

"Forget what I said."

"I usually do."

"Just make sure that you and Betty are in Riverside Park tonight at eight o'clock sharp. Meet me by the tennis courts. You got it?"

"This better not be one of your crazy plans, Jack."

"Oh, it's crazy, all right. Crazy like a fox."

Monday, October 7, 8:00 p.m.
Riverside Park, The Tennis Courts

KC arrived with Betty, right on time. I stepped out of the shadows and onto the path.

"I don't understand what's going on, Jack," Betty said. "Why are we here? Lance is innocent."

"Yeah," KC said, "what are we doing here, Lime? I'm freezing."

"I'll explain everything, but we can't talk out in the open," I said. "Just follow me."

They didn't look happy about it, but they both followed me off the path and back into the shadow of a large tree.

"Now will you tell us what's going on?" KC said.

"I just wanted to make sure we were all in place when he arrived," I said.

"When who arrived?" Betty asked.

"Betty, very shortly your boyfriend, Lance Munroe, is going to come walking down that path."

"What? Why?" she asked.

"Why? Because he got a text message from a guy named Mike the Bookie telling him that there was a dodgeball game going on tonight and that they needed his services."

"Who's *they*, Jack?" KC asked.

"The Riverside Boys," I said.

"He's not in a gang!" Betty said. "He was just helping a friend! Let's go, KC," she added, and marched back out onto the path. My whole plan would've been blown if Lance hadn't come strolling down the path at that exact moment.

"Betty, what are you doing here?" he asked, staggering backward like he'd been punched in the nose.

"She's here because I asked her to be here," I said, bounding onto the path beside Betty. "What are you doing here, Lance?"

"I ... I ..." he stammered.

"I'll tell you what you're doing here," I said. "You're here because you got a text from Mike the Bookie, a known affiliate of the Riverside Boys, telling you to be here. You're here because you're Bucky King's lackey, just another thug working for the Riverside Boys. Isn't that right, Lance?"

"It's not true, Betty."

"He's lying," I said. "He's lying, just like he lied to you about being down here the other night to help out a few friends. I can prove everything!"

"Oh, Lance!" Betty said, through tears.

"Betty, Betty!" Lance cried, running over to her. "I got myself in too deep. Oh, Betty, I've made a mess of things! I didn't mean to hurt you."

"What's going on, Lime?" KC asked.

"He's been cheating on you, Betty," I said, ignoring KC. "He's been cheating on you so that he can take orders from Bucky King and his gang of thieves."

"You got it wrong, Lime," Lance said. "I'm not a member of the Riverside Boys. I just lost a little money playing dodgeball. I got a little carried away, but I figured I could win it back. After all, I'm Lance Munroe, right? And I will win it back, Betty. But in the meantime, Mike said he could keep Bucky off my back if I did him a few favors. So I lost a few dodgeball games. It's no big deal."

"What about the football game on Friday? Don't tell me you didn't plan those last-minute high jinks," I said.

"I'd never lose a football game on purpose. That'd hurt my chances of getting picked up by a top-flight college, but I said I could make it look like we'd lose. Then we're all winners, right? You get to watch a super-exciting game and I get to look even better than I already am."

"That's very noble," I muttered, "but what about the kids who lost their dough betting on that game?"

"Nobody forced them to bet their money, Lime. It's their own fault."

"You lied to me!" Betty cut in. "You told me you were helping out a friend."

"I was helping out me," Lance said.

"That's not the same," Betty cried.

"I'm sorry," Lance said, taking her hands. "I just didn't want you to be worried about me, babe. I wanted to handle it myself. I guess I just got in over my head. I'm really sorry. I just didn't see any other way out."

"Oh, please," I groaned, but Betty bought it hook, line and sinker. Before I could say cheesy, the two of them were kissing and making up.

"How much do you owe them?" KC asked, from out of nowhere.

"About a hundred and twenty-five bucks," Lance said.

"Whoa!" I said. "Hold your horses! You only owe them a hundred and twenty-five bones? You should just go out and get a job; you'd pay that off in no time."

"I don't have time for a job," Lance said. "It's football season."

"I'll lend you the money," Betty said, beaming.

"Well," Lance started, scratching his chin, "now that I'm mixed up in this, Mike says I need to keep playing along. And he's got this little black book filled with bets, and my name's all over the place. He says if I ever change my mind, he'll hand it over to Principal Snit or Coach Shultz, and then I can kiss a big scholarship good-bye. I'm in kind of a tight jam."

"You help get people out of tight jams?" Betty said, looking at me with those big brown eyes.

"No, no, no," I said.

"Oh, please, Jack!" Betty said. "I just know you could help him. Please?"

"That'd be great, Jack! Thanks!" Lance said, patting me on the back. "Some of the fellas on the team said you were a bit of a weirdo, but I always knew you were a stand-up kind of guy."

"Let me get this straight," I said, staring up at Lance. "You got yourself into trouble by losing money on dodgeball games and then tried to work your way out of it by making a deal with the devil instead of getting a job and paying off a hundred and twenty-five bucks? And now, since your name is scrawled all over Mike's little black book, if you don't keep following orders, you might end up losing a sweet football scholarship to a big-time college? And you want me to help you out of this mess?"

Lance and Betty nodded.

"Please, Jack. Please," Betty said, grabbing my hands. I got another whiff of that watermelon bubblegum and my sad fate was sealed.

"Just stay out of my way," I said, heading down the path. "And when this is done," I added, turning around, "each of you owes me a favor. A big one."

They nodded again and I left them standing in the park.

Tuesday, October 8, 4:00 p.m.
29A Main Street, The Diner

When I got to The Diner the next day, Mike was already sitting in the booth at the back, dipping fries into a puddle of ketchup.

"I'm surprised, Lime," he said. "I didn't think you'd show up. Now where's my book?"

"Where's the money for my bike?"

Mike laid out six twenties and a five in a neat line across the table.

"Give me my book," he snapped.

"First, take the money back."

"What?"

"That pays off Lance Munroe's debt, I believe."

"You're joking."

"I'm afraid I'm not," I said. "Take the money and scratch Lance's name out of your book."

"Why would I?"

"Because if you don't, Lance is going to confess everything to Principal Snit and ask for leniency," I said. I was bluffing big time, but he didn't need to know that.

"You're bluffing," he said.

I shrugged and tossed his little black book on the table.

"If Lance squeals, you and Bucky are going down, along with your whole gambling operation. If you let him off the hook, we both walk away from this, and nobody's the wiser."

Mike snatched up the money and the black book.

"You're done with Lance," I said.

"I might be done with Munroe," Mike said, standing up, "but we're just getting started with you, Lime."

Mike stormed out just as KC Stone waltzed in.

"Did I miss something big?" she asked.

"If you had arrived five seconds earlier, Stonc, you would've blown everything."

"Well, I'm glad I have impeccable timing," she said, sliding into the booth. "I don't suppose you want to tell me what just happened? I'm sure it'd make a great story for the paper."

"Sorry," I said. "I didn't do it for the publicity."

"It might help your detective agency," she said. "Attract some business."

"I don't need help with that," I said.

"At least tell me if you managed to get your bike fixed."

"How do you know about that?"

"I'm a journalist, Jack," she said. "I have my ways. Remember?"

I shook my head. "It's still going to need some work."

"I don't suppose you'd like to buy a girl a drink," she said. "It's hot out there today."

"What'll you have?"

"Right about now, I think a root beer float would hit the spot," she said.

I smiled.

"I think we might get along after all," I said.

"Don't bet on it, Lime," she said. "Don't bet on it."

THE CASE OF THE RED ENVELOPE

Thursday, October 10, 8:26 a.m.
Iona High, My Locker

It was a dismal day. It was raining and cold, the kind of cold that seeps under your skin and eats away at your bones. I trudged into school, soaking wet, and headed straight for my locker. I didn't feel much like talking to anyone, especially not KC Stone, but there she was, standing in front of my locker with a waif of a girl who had long black hair and skin so pale that she'd pass for a vampire in downtown Transylvania.

"How's life?" KC asked.

"Wet," I said.

"That's a weather report, Jack. I was wondering how *you're* doing, you know, personally speaking. It's a question polite people ask these days."

"Are you here to give me a lesson on manners, Stone, or is there some other reason why you keep getting in my way?"

"This is Madeleine Summers," she said. "She needs your help, and she needs it fast."

Madeleine blushed and looked down at the ground.

"You know I'm trying to get out of the private-eye racket, right? It's bad for my health and my bank account."

"I wouldn't be here if it wasn't an emergency."

"Maybe this isn't a good idea," Madeleine said, in a whisper.

"Come on, Jack," KC said. "Madeleine is an innocent victim. You can't let something like this happen to her."

"Something like what?" I asked.

KC opened her mouth to explain, but then her eyes darted over my shoulder and she clammed up quick, fast, in a hurry.

"Mr. Lime," a deep voice said from directly behind me.

"Principal Snit," I said, turning around. "What brings you down here this miserable morning?"

"You do," he said. "We need to have a chat, young man."

Whenever Snit uses the words "young" and "man" together, I know there's going to be trouble, so I didn't put up a fight and stepped in line behind him like a good little robot. We didn't get far before KC grabbed my shoulder and spun me around.

"Jack," she said, shoving a phone into my hand, "you must've dropped your cell."

It's a long and sordid story, but I don't own a cell, so her giving me that phone was a bit of a surprise. I decided to play along and see where this was headed.

"Thanks, Stone," I said, "I wouldn't want to go anywhere without this."

"No," she said. "You might miss some very important text messages."

"Just make sure I don't see it or hear it, Mr. Lime," Snit said. "I don't want any interruptions during our meeting."

"I'll be in touch soon," KC said, and she headed back down the hall. I had to hand it to her; KC had a lot of spunk, but that didn't mean I was going to take this case. I had other things to do, like dealing with Snit and that black cloud he had hanging over his head. I had a sneaking suspicion that this meeting wasn't going to be all sunshine and lollipops. And you know what? I was right.

Thursday, October 10, 8:34 a.m.
Iona High, Snit's Office

Snit escorted me to his office and we sat down at his desk.

"Jack, I'm not going to beat around the bush. Yesterday afternoon a student told me that you stole his personal property."

"What?"

"He says that you cornered him in the boys' bathroom and took his diary. He also said you demanded one hundred and twenty-five dollars in order for him to get it back."

"That's ridiculous!" I said, jumping out of my seat. "That's not what happened at all! Mike is lying to you, Mr. Snit!"

"I didn't mention any names, Jack."

"Oh, come on! We both know who we're talking about, and I'm telling you he's lying!"

"So you admit that you cornered Mike Anderson in the boys' bathroom?"

"I wouldn't say he was cornered, exactly," I said.

"Did you steal his diary?"

"Diary? Is that what he's calling it? That's a hoot!"

"Did you take his diary, Jack?"

I wanted to tell Snit the truth, the whole truth and nothing but the truth. I wanted to explain to him that I'd borrowed Mike's betting ledger to save the school's new football hero, Lance Munroe, from Bucky King and the Riverside Boys. But that would mean playing the snitch, and I wasn't willing to do that, even if Mike "The Bookie" Anderson was willing to sink that low.

"I may have momentarily borrowed a small black book that belonged to Mike Anderson," I said, "but I can assure you it wasn't a diary."

"Do you still have it?"

"I gave it back to him on Tuesday."

"That's not what he says."

"He's lying!"

"Did he have to pay you one hundred and twenty-five dollars to get it back?"

"Not exactly," I said. "Kind of. They wrecked my bike!"

"Mike Anderson wrecked your bike, Jack?"

"Did he personally wreck my bike?"

"Yes."

"Probably not, but he knew who did!" I said, pounding the table with my fist.

"So let me get this straight. You admit that you took Mike Anderson's diary —"

"I borrowed a small black book," I said, cutting him off.

"You admit that you took Mike Anderson's personal property and demanded he pay you in order to get it back?"

"Sure, I did those things, but I did them to protect a client and get some payback for some seriously rotten things that were done to *my* innocent bicycle."

"Jack, you can't forcibly take another student's personal property and then demand money for its return. I'm hereby putting you on a one-week, in-school suspension, to begin immediately. And then this matter will be handed over to a disciplinary committee that will determine whether a more serious punishment is warranted."

"A more serious punishment?"

"This isn't a joke, Jack. You could be expelled."

"Don't I at least get a chance to face my accuser?"

"That's not how this works. And, Jack, you are not permitted to speak to Mike Anderson in any way. You are to stay away from him. Are we clear on that?"

"Crystal," I said.

"Good," he said, standing up, "then follow me. I'll show you to your quarters."

Thursday, October 10, 8:44 a.m.
Iona High, My Cell

Snit walked me to a charming room just off the main office. It was a little bigger than a broom closet and tastefully furnished with a rickety old chair, a table, a computer from the 1980s and a pile of science textbooks that looked like they'd been eaten by a great white shark and then spit back into the sea.

"I'm going to get your work from your teachers," Snit said. "And don't think about leaving, Jack. Just consider this your classroom for the week."

"No problemo," I said. "It'll give me a nice break from nasty distractions like windows and people."

Snit glowered and left, shutting the door behind him.

I was itching to track down Mike and share a few kind words, but Snit probably had the office locked down tighter than a Doberman at a kitten convention, so I decided to turn my attention to Madeleine's case instead. I checked KC's phone. She hadn't wasted any time texting me a few facts:

> Art exhibit tonight. Madeleine sure to win.
> Her painting stolen from art room last night.
> You need to find it before 7!

An art heist was a new one on me, and I had to admit I was curious about the case, but I'd need a few more facts before I could get started. That was going to be tough while I was locked up like an animal, so I figured the best thing to do was to text KC for some more info. That's when Snit burst back in.

"Mr. Lime," he barked, "hand over that phone."

"Do you know anything about a missing painting?" I asked.

"No more investigations, Jack, not during school hours and especially not while you're serving a suspension."

"The girl's name is Madeleine Somethingorother. Do you have any leads?"

"Give me the phone, Mr. Lime."

"I'm just trying to help somebody out," I said, handing it over. "Besides, what kind of trouble could I get into while I'm locked up?"

"Stick to your schoolwork," Snit said, putting a pile of worksheets on the desk. "Oh, and by the way, you've got someone to keep you company for the day."

That's when things went from bad to worse.

"I believe you already know Bucky King."

I'm not sure what my face looked like when Bucky stepped into that broom closet, but he was grinning from ear to ear.

"Now, boys, I don't want to hear a peep out of this room," Snit said, "and this door stays open at all times."

"Not a peep," Bucky said, brushing past me and taking the only seat in the house. The chair screeched helplessly under his weight.

"I'll get you another chair," Snit said, and then he left us alone.

"What are you in for, Bucky — stealing candy from babies again, or were you just ripping their teddy bears apart?"

"I'll be tearing somebody apart soon," he said, jumping up and grabbing me by the collar.

Before I had a chance to risk my life with a witty reply, Mr. Van Kramp stepped into our cell, pushing a cushy-looking leather chair on wheels.

Van Kramp had replaced Ms. Priggs as the school secretary after she retired last year. He bicycled to work every day, coached the boys' soccer team and was supposedly an expert mountain climber. He had blue eyes and straw-blond hair that always looked like it'd just been cut. He spoke with a British accent and had a habit of walking around in expensive-looking suits that made me wonder just how much a school secretary got paid. Since Van Kramp had arrived on campus, the girls at Iona High seemed to be spending a lot more time in the office.

"I hate to interrupt," he said, "but Mr. Snit asked me to bring you another chair."

"Thanks," Bucky said, letting me go and grabbing the chair from Van Kramp.

"You're very welcome," Van Kramp said, "and let's keep the noise down, chaps. I have work to do."

"Not a peep," Bucky said. Van Kramp smiled, flashing us his ridiculously white teeth, and left.

Bucky dragged his comfortable new seat over to the desk, kicked the old one into the corner and laid his head down on the desk.

"Don't wake me up unless Snit's on his way. Got it, Lime?"

I figured the old chair Bucky had been using was about ready to fall to pieces, so I sat down on the ground and started hatching my escape plan. The good news was that there were only two things standing in my way. The bad news was that those two things were Mr. Snit and Mr. Van Kramp.

Thursday, October 10, 9:28 a.m.
Iona High, My Cell

Being in the detective game means I solve tricky problems for a living, so it didn't take me long to figure out a way to bust out of this Popsicle stand. I just had to make sure the timing was right. I waited until first period was about to end and then rolled into action.

"Mr. Van Kramp," I said, poking my head out the door, "I need to pee, and fast, or there's going to be a big mess in here."

Van Kramp stopped typing and looked at me like I'd just done my business on his shoes. "Be quick about it," he grumbled, and then went back to work.

I ran out of the office and made my way to the main foyer. The bell rang just as I arrived, and kids started streaming out of their classes. I leaned against the far wall and waited for KC Stone to wander by. I didn't have to wait long.

"Let's walk and talk," I said, sliding up beside her.

"What did Snit want?" KC asked.

"Mike the Bookie is dragging my name through the mud. He told Snit I swiped his diary and then forced him to pay a wad of dough to get it back. What a bunch of baloney."

"Did you do those things?" KC asked.

"Of course I did!" I yelled. "But it wasn't a diary, it was a betting ledger, and I used the cash to help save Lance's Munroe's golden derriere."

"So what now?" she asked.

"Now I'm under lock and key in the main office for a week, which means it's going to be hard to solve this case without a little help."

"What can I do?"

"I need info."

"Fire away."

"Was the door to the art room locked last night?"

"Absolutely," KC said. "I asked the art teacher myself. She said she put the paintings in the supply room at four-thirty yesterday afternoon and locked the door behind her. This morning when she opened the supply room, Madeleine's painting was gone."

"Were any other paintings stolen?"

"Nope."

"Any suspects? Anyone who would want Madeleine out of the way?"

"I asked Madeleine the same thing. She thinks a guy named Sebastian Cain would probably win if she's out of the contest."

"Why would he want to win so bad? What's on the line?"

"The winner is picked by a bunch of profs from the art college in the city. Whoever wins first prize is guaranteed a spot at the college next fall. Plus, Luxemcorp features the winner in their monthly business magazine and puts the artwork on display at the art gallery on Main Street. It's big-time exposure, Jack."

"Anything else you need to tell me, KC?"

"I don't think so," she said. "By the way, where's my phone? I need it back."

"You'll have to ask Snit," I said. "He has a problem with students using phones during suspension."

"Why don't you do it for me," she said with a crooked smile. "He's right behind you."

Thursday, October 10, 9:39 a.m.
Iona High, My Cell

Bucky was still asleep on the desk when Snit and I walked back in.

"Rise and shine, Mr. King," Snit barked, slamming a stack of worksheets on the desk.

"It wasn't me," King mumbled, sitting up.

"I'm sure it wasn't," Snit said with a cold smile. "But perhaps you should start catching up on your work instead of your sleep. And thanks to Mr. Lime, you won't be allowed out of here without an escort. If you need to use the bathroom, gentlemen, you'll have to ask Mr. Van Kramp if he can spare some time."

Snit stalked out, and Bucky handed over the pile of worksheets that Snit had left on the desk.

"You heard the man," he said, tossing them on the floor, "get to work, Limey."

"I'll get to it," I said, "but first I want to know if you've ever heard of a cat named Sebastian Cain."

"Don't know him."

"What about an art heist, Bucky? Have any of your lackeys been busy stealing paintings?"

"Yeah," he said with a chuckle, "Bucky King is real big into paintings. Me and the boys are having a sale down by the river tonight. Black tie. Why don't you drop by and take a look around."

"Thanks for the invite, but I think I'll pass."

"Then stop your yakking. I had a late night."

My gut was telling me I was barking up the wrong tree. Unless Bucky could sell what he stole for a tidy stack of cash, he wasn't interested. Even an award-winning painting wasn't going to fetch much dough on the Iona High black market. So I sat down in the corner and tried to come up with a new way to get out of this hole.

Thursday, October 10, 11:50 a.m.
Iona High, My Cell

All the snoring Bucky was doing got to me after a while, so I decided to catch a little shut-eye myself, just to freshen up, you understand. Unfortunately, I didn't wake up until the lunch bell rang, and I still wasn't any closer to solving this case. I couldn't do that without gathering some more info, and I couldn't do that until I got out of this joint. Lucky for me, Bucky woke up, too.

"Van Kramp!" he yelled, stepping out of our cell. "I need to use the john."

"Fine," Van Kramp said, "come with me. I need to get something to eat anyway."

Sometimes you have to be grateful for what you've got, even if the only thing you've got is Bucky King and his full bladder. I waited a few seconds and then peeked out. The main office was empty and Snit's door was shut, which usually meant he was meeting with someone important. So, like a good little jailbird, I grabbed my opportunity, slipped outside and headed for the cafeteria.

Thursday, October 10, 11:52 a.m.
Iona High, The Cafeteria

I snuck in the back way and spotted KC sitting at a table with Madeleine and a couple of other kids. Van Kramp was busy ordering something to eat at the front counter, so I slunk up to KC's table and sat down.

"Lime," KC said, "I didn't think Mr. Snit would let you out for lunch."

"He didn't," I said, hunching down a little as Van Kramp turned and walked out of the cafeteria. "I don't have much time, so we need to talk fast. Has Cain done anything suspicious?"

"I don't know," KC said. "I haven't monitored Cain's every move, what with school going on and all. But we found this stuck to Madeleine's locker," she added, handing over a red envelope.

I gave it a quick once-over. It was your standard envelope, except for the fact that it was red. There was a piece of tape still stuck to the top. I assumed it'd been used to stick the envelope onto Madeleine's locker. There was another piece of tape on the back that'd been used to seal it shut.

"Are you planning on dusting it for fingerprints?" KC said. "Or are you going to read what's inside?"

"That's what separates the amateurs from the pros, Stone," I said, holding the envelope up so that KC could see the back. "Whoever stuck this to Madeleine's locker doesn't like to lick envelopes."

"Wow," KC said, "I stand corrected, Lime. The envelope is important! Now we just need to question every student at school and find out who doesn't like licking envelopes."

"It's a clue," I growled.

"A lame clue," KC said. "Why don't you just read the letter?"

I opened the envelope and pulled out a plain white sheet that had been folded twice. It read, "Put $50 in this envelop. put it under the last seat on the left, on the last car of the 5 pm train into the city. If you do this I'll call the pay phone near the restrooms at the train station at 5:15 and tell you wear you can find the painting. If you don't, I'll destroy the painting!!!!!!!!!!!!!!!!!!!!"

"What do you think, Lime?" KC asked.

"I think that whoever wrote this note really likes using exclamation points."

"Hardee-har-har," KC said. "What else?"

"It was printed in the library," I said.

"How do you know that?" KC asked.

"Can you see the faint ink smudge running down the left side?" I said, showing the note to everyone at the table. "The printer in the library leaves that smudge behind every time."

Judging by their reactions, the others were impressed by that little bit of detective work.

"Plus, I'd say the perp was in a hurry."

"Because of the spelling mistakes?" KC asked.

"Exactly," I said. "KC, you're getting better at this all the time. Pretty soon you'll be able to solve crimes all by yourself."

"Keep talking like that, Jack, and the next big mystery at this school will be you disappearing forever," she said, glaring at me.

That's when Van Kramp walked back into the cafeteria and started snooping around.

"I don't have time for your gum slapping, Stone," I said, slipping off my chair and squatting beside the table. "Give me a phone, quick, so I can stay in touch."

"Mr. Snit still has mine," KC said.

"You can have mine," Madeleine said, reaching into her pocket.

"No, take mine," another kid said. He was a big guy with brown hair that hung down to his shoulders. "This way you can contact Madeleine yourself. Her number's on my phone. Just make sure you find that painting, okay?"

"Thanks," I said, and slipped his phone into my pocket. I jumped up and was about to make a clean getaway when my grandma and Mr. Snit came through the doorway.

"Jack! Eric! Lime! What! Do you think! You're doing!"

"Grandma," I said, "why are you here?"

"I think you know why I'm here," she said, and then she turned and marched out of the cafeteria.

"Let's go back to my office, Mr. Lime," Mr. Snit said. "I think we need to go over a few things."

Thursday, October 10, 12:07 p.m.
Iona High, Snit's Office

Apparently my grandmother was the important person that Snit had been talking to when I slipped out of my cell. Apparently he called her in to discuss the false accusations of physical intimidation and theft that had been flung in my direction by Mike the Bookie. Apparently she wasn't too happy about the whole situation.

"If you don't mind, Mr. Snit," my grandma said through gritted teeth, "let's hear what Jack has to say."

Snit nodded. "Go ahead, Jack."

"You want to know what I have to say? I say I'm the thorn in the side of every two-bit crook and criminal this side of the Iona River. I say the grifters and goons in our little burg are getting tired of me ruining their plans, so they're starting to point their crooked fingers in my direction. I say that the dirty rotten scoundrel who's behind these charges is bitter because I hurt his gambling operation. I say you cut me loose and this problem will be solved faster than you can say slander."

"Jack," Grandma said, "you're telling me that you didn't steal anything?"

"I didn't steal anyone's diary," I said. "I might've temporarily taken some incriminating information out of the hands of a blackmailer, but I only did that to protect a client."

"Who was your client, Jack?" Snit asked. "Maybe they can corroborate your story."

"I'm afraid I can't tell you that, Mr. Snit. They have to remain anonymous."

"Jack!" Grandma yelled. "It's not your job to protect everyone at Iona High. And you can't sit here and tell me that you only borrowed something. Stealing is stealing."

"I gave it back," I said. "Just like I said I would."

"No!" Grandma said, leaping up. "This will not do! You did something wrong, and I will not sit here and argue with you about it. Mr. Snit, I'll leave this in your hands. If you think that Jack should be expelled, and I wouldn't be surprised if you did, I will stand by your decision. As for you, Jack, you're to follow orders and do your work. If I hear that you're involved in one of your cases, you'll be spending the rest of the year receiving your education at home, with me. Do you understand?"

"Homeschooled? With you? You can't be serious, Grandma?"

Grandma's eyes got so big that I thought they might shoot out of her head like some cartoon character.

"Oh, I'm serious, Jack," she said. "And do you know what the great thing about being homeschooled is?"

"You get to sleep in?" I said.

"No," she said, smiling, "it's that school never ends. You won't have time for anything else, just school, day after day after day. Do you understand?"

"I understand," I said.

"Thank you, again, for coming in to see me, Mrs. Lime," Snit said, standing up.

"Not at all," she said, shaking his hand and heading for the door, but she stopped before she left. "Jack," she said, "aren't you going to walk me out?"

"Of course," I croaked. The front doors at Iona High are only a hop, skip and a jump from Snit's office, but I had a feeling this was going to be a very long walk.

Thursday, October 10, 12:28 p.m.
Iona High, The Main Foyer

As I predicted, Grandma and I had a lovely stroll to the main doors. While we walked, she helped me imagine, in great detail, exactly what it would be like working from sunup to sundown in the comfort of our front room while she watched me do my reading, writing and arithmetic problems over and over again. She left and I headed back to the office. Unfortunately Mike the Bookie stepped in front of me with a kid who had blond hair, big blue eyes and who was wearing a red golf shirt with the collar popped up.

"Jack," Mike said, "was that your grandmother?"

"She always comes here for lunch on Thursdays, Mike," I said. "We sit down with Snit and make a list of who's been naughty and who's been nice. And guess what? You made the naughty list this week."

"What about my friend here? Is he on the naughty list, too?"

"I don't know, who's your friend?"

"This is Sebastian Cain."

Cain smiled. "I've heard a lot about you, Lime. None of it's been good."

"Figures the two of you would be best buddies," I said. "Well, you're not going to get away with it."

"Get away with what?" Mike asked.

"You're not going to get away with your little diary scam, Mike," I said, "and Cain's not going to get away with stealing Madeleine's painting."

"I don't know what you're talking about," Cain said, chuckling.

"And even if we did know," Mike added, "nobody's going to listen to you, Jack, especially not Snit."

"We'll see who's listening to me at the end of the day, Mikey."

"Sure we will," Mike said. "But I want you to know, Jack, that Sebastian's dad is a bigwig with Luxemcorp."

"A seriously big bigwig," Cain added.

"And once he hears that you pushed me around and stole my diary, he's going to make sure you get kicked out of Iona High," Mike said. "Our school doesn't need any more thugs."

"No, Mike, you got that covered, don't you?"

"Why don't you run along and go play detective," Cain said, stepping up to me. "Just don't be surprised if you're not back on Monday."

I grabbed Cain by his red collar and pulled him close. "Don't think you're walking away with any prizes tonight, Sebastian. I'm going to be on you like a wet sweater on a gorilla. You got that, pal-o? I'm taking you down."

"You'll never find that painting before tonight," Cain hissed. "I guarantee it."

"That ransom note was just a diversion, wasn't it?"

He smirked.

"Tell me where it's at," I growled, "or you're going to be in for a world of hurt."

"What are you going to do? Call your parents? Oh wait, they're dead, aren't they?"

I was close to doing something I was really going to regret, when our little party was rudely interrupted.

"Let him go, Mr. Lime!" Van Kramp ordered.

Cain winked and I knew I'd been duped. They wanted to get under my skin, and I was silly enough to let them do it. Now I was trapped. I saw Van Kramp hauling me into Snit's office. I saw Snit calling my grandma. I saw years of homeschooling stretching out in front of me.

"Let him go!" Van Kramp repeated.

I was just relaxing my grip when, for the first time ever, my condition kicked in at exactly the right moment.

Thursday, October 10, ?:?? p.m.
Sleepy Land, Jack's Dream

I dreamed I was at the train station, standing beside a pay phone that was ringing. I picked it up.

"Hello?"

"Jack?"

"Yeah, who's this?"

"It's KC."

"What do you want now?"

"It's a setup, Jack. They're setting you up again."

"Who's setting me up?"

"Don't go snooping around this place, Jack. And whatever you do, don't answer any phones."

"It's too late," I said. "I'm talking to you on a phone."

"No you're not," she said.

I spun around and there she was, standing behind me, wearing a big white poufy dress. A shiny black train was on the tracks behind her. The windows were filled with shadowy figures.

"Who's setting me up?" I asked again.

"Just don't come back to the station," she said, and then she whirled around and ran onto the train.

"Wait!" I called, but the doors shut and the train rumbled away.

That's when I woke up.

Thursday, October 10, 12:47 p.m.
Iona High, The Main Foyer

I was surrounded by a small mob of gawkers and slack jaws, all staring down at me. Van Kramp was trying to hustle them away while Snit kneeled beside me and looked concerned.

"Are you okay, Jack?" he asked. His breath reeked of coffee.

"I think so," I said, sitting up.

"Take it easy," Snit said. "You've been asleep for almost ten minutes."

"I'm fine," I said. "I'm just hungry."

"Victor," Snit said, turning to Van Kramp, "could you go get him a sandwich from the cafeteria, please."

Van Kramp nodded and left. I stood up and scanned the crowd for Mike or Cain, but they must've scrammed when I went down.

"Let's get back to the office," Snit said, and he pushed his way through the crowd. We got inside and he led me back to my cell, but before he opened the door, he stopped and said, "Mr. Van Kramp told me about you and Sebastian Cain, Jack, but I'm going to do you a favor and pretend it never happened. However, I'm warning you, young man, if you stick even a toe out of the detention room for the rest of the day, I'm calling your grandmother. Have you got that?"

"Loud and clear," I said.

"Not a single solitary toe," he said, wagging his finger in my face.

"Not even my little one," I promised and he opened the door to my cell. Bucky was still inside, snoring away on the desk.

"Wake up!" Snit yelled as I strolled in.

Bucky sat up and looked around. "Is it over?"

"Not yet, Mr. King," Snit said. "And I expect to see

some work done by the two of you before you leave."

Snit left and I took a seat on the floor.

"Getting into trouble again, Limey?" Bucky asked, and yawned.

"Finding things out is more like it. I don't suppose I could pay you to ask a few questions for me? You know, use your muscle to get some answers?"

"Pay me with what, Lime? A favor?"

That's when Van Kramp came in with my sandwich.

"Feeling better?" he asked.

"Just peachy," I said.

"Good, then there's no reason why the two of you should bother me for the rest of the day, correct?"

"Correct," Bucky said, eyeing my sandwich.

Van Kramp left and Bucky headed my way.

"You look pretty hungry, Bucky. I could pay you with this sandwich?"

"You're going to give me that sandwich anyway, Lime."

"I don't think so," I said, standing up. Bucky stared down at me and I heard his big knuckles cracking as he curled his hands into fists.

"You're a real tough guy, ain't you, Limey?"

"No tougher than anyone else," I said. "I'm just not afraid of getting hurt."

"Over a sandwich?"

"It's not about the sandwich," I said, "and we both know it."

Bucky laughed. It sounded like a buzz saw cutting through wood.

"You're a real piece of work," he said, leaning in. I got my face ready for something bad to happen, but Bucky just turned around and sat back down in his cushy chair.

I breathed again, unwrapped the sandwich and handed him half.

"My mother always taught me to share," I said.

"You're a real piece of work," he said again. "You know I almost rearranged your face just now?"

"That's what I like about you, Bucky. I always know where I stand. There are some people out there, well, you just can't tell what they're going to do next."

"People got a lot of different reasons to do things. Me, I do things for the money. It's the only reason to do anything anyway."

Bucky was wrong about that, but I wasn't going to debate him. I barely survived the sandwich incident and didn't want to push my luck. Instead I turned my attention to the pile of work sitting beside me on the floor. If I busted my hump, I could get it all done before the final bell. That way Snit wouldn't waste time raking me over the coals at the end of the day for slacking off, and I could track down my new BFF, Sebastian Cain.

"Thanks for the sandwich, Limey," Bucky said. "Now keep your trap shut. I'm going back to sleep."

"Sweet dreams, Bucky," I said, and got busy solving some math problems.

Thursday, October 10, 3:05 p.m.
Iona High, The Main Foyer

When the final bell rang, Snit stalked in, looking stern, and I shoved my work in his hands. He gave it a quick once-over and nodded.

"I'll see you back here tomorrow morning, Mr. Lime, bright and early," he said, and I made a break for it.

I sprinted past Van Kramp before he had a chance to look up from his computer and headed straight for the main foyer. I took up position in the far corner and kept my eyes peeled for Cain. Unfortunately, while I was busy trying to stay under the radar, KC and Madeleine strolled over.

"Any luck with the case, Jack?" KC asked.

"Keep it down, Stone," I hissed. "I'm on a stakeout here."

"Oh, sorry," she said, looking around, "I forgot you like to hide out in the open like this."

"Say whatever it is you came to say and vamoose."

"I don't suppose all this sneaking around out in the open has anything to do with Madeleine's case?"

"I got a news flash for you, Stone. Sebastian Cain is your man. He practically confessed," I said. "I just need to track him down before he leaves."

"That shouldn't be hard, even for you. He's right over there," she said, hiking her thumb over her shoulder.

She was right; Cain was standing on the other side of the foyer.

"What's your plan?" she asked.

"I'm going to follow Cain. He's either going to lead me to that painting or I'm going to make him tell me where it is."

"That's very clever, Jack, and I'm sure it's all going to work out, but Madeleine's decided she's going to pay the ransom. Maybe, after you're done with Cain, you could meet us at the train station to make sure everything goes smoothly."

"That's a mistake," I said, watching Cain head for the front doors. "He's not going to give you that painting, even if you pay. I'd be surprised if he ever planned to collect the ransom in the first place. It's all just a ploy to keep us busy until he's got the blue ribbon pinned on his lapel."

"Just the same, Lime," KC said, "we'll be at the train station if you need us."

"Then that's where I'll deliver the painting when I get it," I said. "Now if you'll excuse me, I've got a nasty flimflam man to follow."

Thursday, October 10, 4:38 p.m.
The Steppes, The Cain Place

Cain wasn't in a hurry, that's for sure. He wandered down Main Street, stopping a couple of times to check his cell. Then he strolled over to Monty's Café, ordered a drink (probably something frothy and expensive) and sat down in one of their puffy leather sofas. I waited down the street and pretended to window-shop for shoes. After forty-five minutes the owner came out and asked me why I was spending so much time outside a women's shoe store. I told her I was just doing a little market research. She didn't buy it and asked me to move along. It was starting to get a little chilly, so I ducked into The Diner and grabbed a good old-fashioned cup of joe. When I came out, Cain was on the move again.

After a leisurely jaunt down Main, he crossed the bridge and walked into Riverside Park. I was starting to smell an ambush, but I couldn't turn back now, so I followed him in. After half an hour of admiring the leaves in the park, Cain headed out; no ambush, no secret meetings, no painting. It was already 4:38 when he picked up the pace and went back across the bridge. He booted across Main Street, down Milky Way Boulevard and into the ritzy part of town known as The Steppes. I followed him past one giant McMansion after another until he stepped off the sidewalk and ambled across the perfectly mowed lawn of a ridiculously large brick house.

I checked my watch — 4:45. I had fifteen minutes before the alleged drop at the train station. Cain wandered around to the back, and I crept to the corner of the house. Cain stepped up to a garage and entered the security code. The door slid up, almost silently, and Cain went inside. Seconds later he came back out carrying a black garbage bag that contained something square and flat. Either he was throwing out a very large book or he had Madeleine's painting in that bag. It was time to make my move.

When he got within ten feet of me, I bolted around the corner and threw myself at him like a battering ram. Cain crumpled and the painting went flying.

"Caught! Red-handed!" I yelled, pinning him down.

"Doing what?" Cain said, struggling to get his arms free.

"Still playing the dumb mug, eh?" I said. "Well, why don't we have a little look at what's inside that bag?"

"Go ahead!"

"Don't make any sudden movements, Cain," I said, letting him go and standing up.

"I've got no reason to run," he said, sweeping his hair into place.

I strode over to the bag and pulled out the painting. It was a red triangle on a white canvas. The lines were thick, and at each of the three points the paint had dripped down the canvas like blood. Cain's signature was scrawled in the bottom corner in the same red paint.

"I think I'll call it *The Idiot*, after you, Lime," Cain said with a smirk.

"What are you talking about?"

"Did you enjoy the leaves in the park? They're so pretty this time of year, aren't they?"

"Where's the painting?" I said.

"I don't know," he said, still sitting on the ground. "Mike told me this morning that it'd been stolen or something. We thought it might be funny to string you along. Mike said you'd fall for it. I guess he was right, huh?"

"Where is Mike, anyway?"

"He had some other business he had to take care of," Cain said.

"I bet he did," I said, and checked my watch. It was 4:52. I had eight minutes to get to the train station. The odds were against me, but since when do I pay attention to the odds?

"Very clever plan," I said, tossing his painting on the lawn. "You divert my attention while Mike makes the drop. I should've known better! But don't start patting yourself on the back yet. It's just a matter of time before I pin it on you."

"You've got nothing, Lime."

I was going to hammer him with a witty comeback but thought I'd better save my breath. I bolted out of his driveway and started sprinting down the street. If only I had my bike, I might've had a chance to make it before the five o'clock train rolled out.

Thursday, October 10, 5:05 p.m.
2 Main Street, The Train Station

I ran as hard as I could and I still missed the drop. I stumbled onto the platform just as the train was pulling out of the station. My lungs were burning, and I was soaked with sweat. I leaned over on my knees, sucking in air and thought about throwing up. That's when I noticed KC, Madeleine and their long-haired friend who had given me his phone heading my way. Despite this catastrophe, they were all smiles.

"Julian saved the day!" KC exclaimed, as they walked over to me.

"What?" I asked.

"He got my painting back," Madeleine said, smiling at the long-haired kid.

She held up a painting that was a mash of different shades of green all swirling together on a canvas that was a little smaller than a placemat. Across the middle was a diagonal line of black that cut the painting in two.

"It's called *Wasteland*," Madeleine said, beaming at Julian.

"How?" I said, still trying to catch my breath.

"It was easy," Madeleine said. "I just experimented with different shades of green and —"

I held up my hand and cut her off. "No ... how did you ... get the painting?"

"I knew about the ransom note," Julian said, "so I decided to come here a little early to see if I could catch the thief in action."

"And guess what, Jack?" KC said, slapping me on the back. "He did!"

"I just got lucky," Julian said, shrugging. "He was coming out of the bathroom with the painting. I grabbed it and he ran away."

"Who?" I asked.

"I don't know," Julian said. "He was wearing a mask."

"Are you okay, Jack?" KC asked. "Why are you so sweaty?"

"I'll tell you another time," I said.

"Well, why don't you come back to the school with us? We're all going to help get ready for the big show tonight," KC said. "I'm sure Madeleine would love to have you there, even if you didn't solve the mystery."

Madeleine smiled and nodded.

"I need a drink first," I said. "And then a very long shower."

"We'll see you later, then," KC said, and they all left me standing at the station.

I wiped my brow and headed for the exit. It'd been a long day. I needed time to think and a tall, frosty root beer float.

Thursday, October 10, 5:51 p.m.
29A Main Street, The Diner

I spent my time at The Diner sipping on my float and mulling over what just happened. Cain and Mike the Bookie had played me like a fiddle and I'd squeaked out all the right notes. I finished my float and decided to look into this mess later. It was time to go home and get some real grub. Tonight was meatloaf night, my favorite night of the week, but when I reached for my wallet, I realized I still had Julian's phone in my pocket. I knew he was back at the school, helping Madeleine get set up for the art exhibit, so I figured the gentlemanly thing to do was to return it ASAP. Especially since he'd managed to save the day, no thanks to me, of course.

Thursday, October 10, 6:27 p.m.
Iona High, The AV Room

A kid named Ernie pointed me in the direction of the AV room when I asked where I could find Julian. There was the usual group of teachers and students scurrying around, trying to spruce up the school before the VIPs arrived, so nobody took any notice of yours truly waltzing in. Julian was rushing around, too, and he came whipping out of the AV room at the same time that I was walking in. We ended up on the floor with the stack of papers he'd been carrying floating down around us like giant snowflakes.

"Sorry about that," Julian said, jumping up and starting to collect the papers.

"My fault," I said, picking up a few sheets, too. They had big black arrows on them with the words "ART EXHIBIT" underneath. I also found a giant-sized key ring, packed with keys, under a couple of pages and handed them over. "You must have every key in the school on that."

"Part of the job of being in charge of the audiovisual equipment," he said, taking the keys from me.

I helped him gather up the rest of the papers and gave him the phone. "I figured you might want this back."

"Thanks," he said. "Sorry I can't talk, Jack, but I have to get these posters up before the judges arrive."

"No problemo," I said, and he hustled down the hallway.

I considered staying for the show but decided I didn't want to miss Grandma's meatloaf, not after the day I'd just had. Plus, I needed a shower. On my way out, I met the first guest coming in. He was about four feet tall and looked like he might be celebrating his hundredth birthday sooner than later. I held the door open and he handed me a red envelope.

"What's this?" I asked, a little surprised, since it looked exactly like the envelope that had been stuck to Madeleine's locker.

"My ticket is inside! I'm Dr. Nessling!" he barked, taking off his black fedora and pointing at the envelope. His name was written in fancy looping script across the front. "I'm one of the judges! Take me to the gym!"

"Follow the arrows," I said, pointing at the signs Julian had just put up. The black arrows clearly showed the way toward the gym.

"What!" he yelled, looking at me like I'd just suggested he go jump in a lake.

"Or you can follow me," I said, and escorted him down to the gym. Ms. Henny, the art teacher, marched over as soon as we arrived and I excused myself.

"You should get a better doorman!" the good doctor yelled, and I exited stage right.

On my way out, I stopped in front of one of the signs with the black arrows. It had a smudge along the left side, just like the ransom note, which meant it must've been printed in the library, too. That's when I actually managed to have a bright idea. It occurred to me that Ms. Slits, the librarian, required students entering the library to jot down their names and note the time of their entry on one of her sign-in sheets. And Ms. Slits was a stickler about those sheets. There's no way you could slip in under an assumed name — believe me, I've tried a few times.

If I could peruse those sign-in sheets, I might be able to narrow down who'd been using the computers around the time that the ransom note had been stuck to Madeleine's locker. And since Julian had the keys to every room in the school, I might actually be able to get some proof that tied Cain and Mike to the art heist. Then I could stop Cain from competing in tonight's extravaganza and all would be right in the world. I just had to track down Julian.

So I headed back to the AV room. The light was on and the door was open, but Julian wasn't there. I figured he'd be back soon and I grabbed a seat. While I waited I glanced at the computer monitor and noticed that there was a pop-up on the screen notifying him that something had just finished printing in the library. I figured that's where he was, so I made a beeline for the library and arrived just as he was stepping out the door.

"I need to have a look at Ms. Slits's sign-in sheets," I said, squeezing past him.

"I don't think that's a good idea," Julian said, following me back inside.

"Don't worry about it," I said with a wink. "I won't tell if you won't."

"Really, Jack," he said, "I'm not supposed to let anyone else in here."

"It'll only take a second," I said, grabbing the sign-in book from Slits's desk and opening it up. I scanned the sign-in sheet from the time the library opened at 8:17 a.m.

until noon, but Cain's name wasn't there, and neither was Mike's.

"No luck?" Julian asked.

"Maybe they connected to the library printer from some other computer," I said.

"Well, if anyone can track him down, Jack, it's you."

"I don't know," I said as we walked out. "I'm starting to wonder about that."

"I guess you just have to follow the clues, right?" Julian said, locking the door behind us.

"That's a good piece of advice," I said. "And thanks for letting me in."

"Sure, Jack" he said, walking away. "I wish I could help out more, but I've got to run."

Julian was right; I just had to follow the clues. The only problem was that Cain and Mike had covered their tracks better than a snowshoe hare in a blizzard. I was banging my head against a wall and getting nowhere fast, so I decided (for the second time that night) to go home and sleep on it. Unfortunately I met Cain coming in.

"Good luck winning tonight," I said. "I think the judges will be very impressed with a high school student who's able to paint shapes."

"You wouldn't know art if it slapped you in the face, Lime," he said, brushing past me.

"No, but I know a cheater when I see one. Too bad Mike was interrupted in the middle of your ploy. I guess stealing that painting was a big waste of time, huh?"

"For the last time, we didn't steal Madeleine's painting."

"Sure, Cain, you stick to that story. It sounds real cute."

"I thought this might occur to you on your own, Lime, but why would I want to give Madeleine her painting back if I managed to steal it? If I wanted to get her out of the exhibition tonight, wouldn't I just throw it in the garbage, where it belongs?"

"Funny," I said, "I've been thinking the same thing about you all day."

"Yeah, I have to go now, but I'll be at Monty's Café tomorrow after school, Jack. Why don't you drop in and buy me a café mocha for winning the grand prize tonight?"

"I'd love to, Cain, except I'm going to be busy twiddling my thumbs."

"I wish I could stay longer and gab about your hobbies, Jack, but I've got a contest to win," he said, and then he turned and left.

I walked out the front doors and back into the crisp October night. Cain was a scoundrel and a rascal, but he made a good point: why not just toss Madeleine's painting in the river? And if he wasn't involved, then Mike probably wasn't involved either. So who was the masked man at the train station? Whoever it was had to have access to the art room and the library printer. Plus, they'd probably be involved in the art exhibit, since they'd used the same type of red envelope for the ransom note that was being used to deliver the art show tickets. And what about motive? Would anyone really go through all that trouble for a measly fifty bucks? Who came out of this big mess smelling like a bunch of daisies? That's when the answer hit me like a bucket of paint landing right on top of my head. I turned around and walked back into Iona High.

Thursday, October 10, 6:58 p.m.
Iona High, The Art Exhibition

When I walked into the gym, Julian was getting a pat on the back from Principal Snit and KC was capturing that magic moment for the *Iona High Guardian*. Madeleine was standing beside her painting, looking pleased as punch with the whole situation. She was wearing a black evening gown with a green shawl draped over her shoulders. Her hair was held up in a loose bun by two black chopsticks, and she'd put on some striking red lipstick that jumped out at you against her pale skin. This was a jazzed-up version of the girl I'd met that morning. Not that there was anything wrong with the girl I'd met earlier, but it helped me understand the motive behind the crime a little bit better.

When KC was done with the photo shoot, she wandered over to me. "Hi Jack," she said, and then took a step back. "Wow, it smells like you didn't have a chance to have that shower."

"I got sidetracked," I said, watching Julian stroll over to Madeleine and her painting. "All done taking pictures of the latest local hero?"

"You're not jealous, are you, Jack?"

"You're joking, right?"

"Well, I think he deserves the recognition. He solved the crime and saved the day."

"There's more to solving a crime than just finding the stolen merchandise. You have to ID the crook, too."

"You've got a lead?" KC asked.

"Maybe," I said, "but I need to ask Julian a few questions before I know the truth."

I left KC and strolled over to Julian and Madeleine who were busy awkwardly staring at each other.

"Julian," I said, "do you think you could let me into the art room?"

"I don't think so, Jack," he said. "I'm only supposed to use those keys for official school business."

"I think there's an important clue that we've missed," I said. "It'll only take me a minute."

Julian looked at Madeleine. She smiled and nodded.

"Okay," he said, leading the way out of the gym. "But it'll have to be quick."

"Quick and painless," I said with a smile. "Well, maybe not painless," I added, but I don't think he heard that part.

Thursday, October 10, 7:11 p.m.
Iona High, The Art Room

Julian opened the door and we both stepped inside.

"Would you mind hitting the lights?" I asked, and Julian switched them on.

"Thanks," I said, "I think this case is officially closed."

"What do you mean?" he asked.

"Well," I started, "I just needed to make sure you had a key to this room. I already knew that you had access to the library printer, and I had a hunch that if I rooted around in that AV room of yours, I'd find a few red envelopes tucked in a desk drawer, or maybe in a filing cabinet?"

"I don't know what you're talking about, Jack."

"I'm talking about you pretending to be some kind of hero, Julian. I'm talking about you sneaking in here and swiping Madeleine's painting. I'm talking about you throwing together a sloppy ransom note and then making up a loopy story about some masked bandit who just handed over his ill-gotten gains without so much as a single punch being thrown. I'm talking about going to Snit right now and setting him straight. That's what I'm talking about, Julian. Now what are you talking about?"

Julian made a break for the door, but I was expecting that kind of lame move. I lowered my shoulder and bodychecked him on the way by. That sent him careening into the corner, and he ended up in a heap on the floor.

"You can't prove anything!" he said, getting back up.

"I know that the computer in the AV room prints to the library. I bet we could check the print jobs that have been sent from that computer and we'd find that ransom note. What do you think, Julian? Should we talk to Snit? Get him to dig around a little bit?"

Julian sat back down in the corner and put his face in his hands. "I didn't want it to come to this," he admitted. "I just wanted to look at her painting, just for one night."

"A likely story," I said. "And then what? You just happened to hatch a fiendish scheme to blackmail your so-called friend and force her to pay fifty bucks to buy her own painting back? Not to mention the fact that you had her worried sick for the whole day! It's time to come clean, Julian. Be honest, who put you up to it? Sebastian Cain? Mike Anderson? Who was it?"

"No!" he yelled. "It's not like that! I just wanted to look at it for the night. After school yesterday I took it home. I meant to bring it back early this morning, but I slept in, and by the time I got here, everyone was talking about how Madeleine's painting had been stolen. I couldn't just bring it back. Then I heard that you'd been hired to solve the case and I came up with the ransom note idea. I thought, maybe, I could solve the case and get the painting back. Then, maybe, she'd notice me. It was a pretty stupid idea, I guess."

"Yeah," I said, "it was pretty stupid."

"Well, at least she's got her painting back. Now she still has a chance to win," he said. "That's the important thing."

"You're probably right," I said.

"Now what?" he asked. "I guess I have to go admit everything to Mr. Snit, huh? But before you haul me in, Jack, give me the chance to talk to Madeleine? I want to tell her the truth myself, okay?"

"I don't think that will be necessary," I said.

"What do you mean?" he asked, standing up.

"I mean, this was a crime of passion," I said, "plain and simple. You did something stupid to impress a girl. I can relate to that, believe me. But you're going to owe me a favor, Julian, and it's going to be a real doozy."

"Oh, thank you, Jack!" he said, hugging me. That's when KC Stone stepped into the room.

"Whoops," she said. "I didn't mean to interrupt something."

"We're just finishing up," I said, pushing Julian away. "And you're not interrupting anything important."

"Thanks, Jack!" Julian said again.

"Forget about it," I said. "Now am-scray before I change my mind."

"Am-what?" he said.

"Get out of here!" I said. Julian didn't need to be told twice.

"I don't suppose you've got anything to put on the record for the newspaper, Lime?" KC asked.

"Not today," I said.

"When you do have something to say," she said, "you'll make sure I'm the first to know, right?"

"Absolutely," I said, stepping into the hall. "Now why don't we get back to that art show?"

"Actually, Jack," she said, "I think you need to go have that shower. You kind of reek."

"Let me know how it all turns out."

"Only if you tell me what just happened here?"

"No can do, kiddo," I said, walking away.

"Fine," she said. "Oh, and Jack, if you call me kiddo again, you'll have more than just some rank BO to worry about."

I walked outside, into a clear autumn night, and felt a little better about the world, even if I did let KC have the last word. All I cared about at that moment was scarfing down some of Grandma's meatloaf and having a long, hot shower. Life was good — for a little while, anyway.

THE COMIC BOOK CAPER

Friday, November 1, 4:21 p.m.
A street with no name, Grandma's House

KC Stone sat at my grandma's kitchen table with a big slice of pumpkin pie, a glass of milk and a notebook lying in front of her. Her red hair was pulled back in a ponytail, and she was wearing a black T-shirt with the words "I'm sorry for your loss, but it's my gain" printed across the front.

"You're sure you want to do this, Lime?" she asked.

"Stone," I said, "you've been hounding me for an interview since I cracked the Richie Renfrew case. Now you're asking me if I'm sure I want to do this?"

"Professional courtesy," she said, pulling a pencil out from behind her ear.

"Where should I start?" I asked, pushing my half-finished float to the side.

"From the very beginning, Jack. How did you get involved with this case?"

"You know how I got involved in this mess," I said.

"For the benefit of my readers," she said with a wink, "just pretend I don't know anything."

"That shouldn't be hard," I said.

"Hardee-har-har. Now quit wasting time and get started."

Wednesday, October 30, 8:19 a.m.
Iona High, My Locker

It all started on Wednesday morning when a scrawny kid with hair so blond that it was almost white walked up to my locker.

"Are you Jack Lime?" he asked. He had big blue eyes that kept darting around, up and down the hall.

"Who's asking?" I said.

"My name's Jake Clim," he said, "and I need help."

"Join the club," I said. "What's the trouble, kid?"

"I'm new around here and a couple of guys, big guys, have been bothering me," he said, his voice trembling a little. "They told me to meet them at the train station at lunch. They said to bring fifty dollars or they'd beat me up."

"And you want me to make them back off?" I said. This kid was small, and I wondered what sort of no-good dirty bum would put the screws to such a helpless sap.

"No," he said, pulling out a small camcorder, "I just want you to come down to the train station today at lunch and record them pushing me around. Then I'll show it to Principal Snit."

"Look," I said, "I've been through this recording bit before, and it doesn't always go down smoothly. Why don't I just have a chat with them, man to thugs?"

"Just take the camera," he said, thrusting it into my

hand. "And get them off my back!"

"You'll owe me a favor for this, kid!" I called, but he was already scurrying away. I grabbed my books from my locker and headed to the cafeteria. I had this figured for just another run-of-the-mill case where an innocent rube gets hustled by some oversized goons, and then yours truly steps in and saves the day. Unfortunately nothing about this case was going to be run-of-the-mill.

Wednesday, October 30, 12:15 p.m.
2 Main Street, The Train Station

It was raining buckets of cats and pails of dogs as I hustled down to the train station. I was soaked when I arrived and slipped into an out-of-the-way corner where I stood dripping and waiting for the goons to show up. I milled around for ten minutes, holding Jake's camera and keeping my eyes peeled for any sign of a shakedown, but nobody showed. I was about to take a stroll around the station to see if I was missing something when Jake came through the front doors. He was wearing a yellow raincoat and holding an umbrella with a duck-shaped handle. No wonder the poor kid was getting hassled.

I waved, and he marched over with short, quick steps, using his umbrella like a cane.

"Give me the camera," he said. "The case is closed."

"What do you mean?" I said. "Did they already get to you?"

"No," he said, grabbing the camera, turning and marching away.

"You still owe me a favor, kid," I called, but he just kept on going. He didn't even look back when he stepped through the doors.

Wednesday, October 30, 12:22 p.m.
Iona High, The Main Foyer

When I got back to school, I was so waterlogged that my fingers had gone wrinkly. I just wanted to dry off and grab something hot to eat in the cafeteria. So I didn't notice the gaggle of guys and dolls standing around in the main foyer, pointing in my direction.

"That's him," someone said.

A kid with black hair almost shaved off and a five o'clock shadow broke out of the crowd. "You Jack Lime?" he barked, stepping up to me.

The kid was built like a pit bull, short and thick, and his beady black eyes were giving me bad vibes.

"That's right," I said.

"Where've you been?" he asked.

"What's it to you, friend?"

"I'll tell you what it is to me," he spat. "My Captain Marvel #146 just got stolen!"

"Your what?"

"My Captain Marvel #146. A very valuable comic book. My very valuable comic book."

"And somebody took it?"

"You got something wrong with your brain, punchy? That's what I just said! Now, what are you going to do about it?"

"I'm guessing you want me to find it," I said.

"You got it right, punchy. So what's it going to be?"

"Who are you, anyway?" I asked.

"Tyler Butt," he said. He looked like he was expecting me to crack a joke, and I have to admit, I had a few snappy comments on the tip of my tongue.

"Give me the facts while I grab some lunch."

"No time for lunch, punchy. Just follow me."

My gut was telling me to walk away from this mooyuk, but I'm a sucker for a good case. So, against my better judgment, I put my lunch plans on hold and started my tragic search for Tyler's missing comic.

"Tragic, Jack?" KC said, looking up from her notepad.

"It was tragic," I said, holding up my hands. "Tragic for me."

"Enough with the dramatics. Just stick with the story, okay?"

Wednesday, October 30, 12:27 p.m.
Iona High, The Gym

Tyler led me to the gym, which was buzzing with students. Tables had been set up along the walls where kids were displaying stacks of comic books. There were even a few people dressed up as their favorite hero. A giant banner was hanging across the stage that read "Welcome to the 1st Annual Iona High Comic-Con." That's when you came up to me, Stone, and said something like, 'Oh, my hero! Thank goodness you're here! I don't know what we'd do without you!'"

"Lime," KC said, looking up again, "if you're not going to take this seriously, I'm out of here and you can deal with the fallout all by yourself."

"Okay, but you have to admit you were happy I showed up."

"Well, I thought you should definitely be involved with this case."

"If getting duped and double-crossed is something I should be involved with, then you were right on the money," I said. "But I'm getting off track. Where was I?"

"You just walked into the gym."

Right, so I suggested we start with the crime scene, and Tyler took me over to his display table. He grabbed a heavy-duty aluminum briefcase, unlocked it with a small key and took out about a dozen old-looking comic books sealed in plastic bags.

"These are all your comics?" I asked, reaching out.

"Don't touch," Tyler barked, stepping between me and his comics. "This is just a small portion of my Captain Marvel collection."

"But only one of them got stolen?" I asked.

Tyler nodded. "The Captain Marvel #146, my most valuable one. The little turd knew what he was doing."

"Why don't you tell me what happened," I said.

"My comic got stolen," Tyler said, his eyes getting wild. "What more do you need to know, punchy?"

I was about to tell Tyler where he could stick his precious Captain Marvel comic when you cut in.

"Tyler, why don't I explain everything to Jack?"

"Fine," he grumbled, "but be quick about it."

We moved to the side, and you explained that the Comic-Con was an event where comic book aficionados could show off their collections and buy and trade with one another. You said you got there at about five to twelve while people were setting up, and that at exactly 12:05 (you knew because you checked your watch), Mariam Singh, the Student Council president, got up on stage to say a few words. That's when the lights went out. About ten seconds later, the lights came on and Tyler pointed at the gym doors and shouted, "There he goes!" You turned and spotted someone dressed in black going out the gym doors. That's when Tyler freaked and tried to go after the crook, only some poor sap got in his way and they both went down in a heap. By the time Tyler got outside, it must've been too late, because he came back empty-handed.

"Is that about right, KC?"

"That's exactly right, Lime. Very impressive."

"Impressive is what I do best," I said.

"Yes, Jack," KC said, "I'm always impressed that you get anything done."

"Thank you," I said, "but we can talk about me later. It wasn't long before Snit arrived and conducted a very thorough investigation that involved asking Tyler questions for about five seconds. Am I missing anything?"

"Just the part about Darla," she said.

"Right, Darla, the newspaper's photographer," I said. "She was short with pink hair and a nose ring. After you finished explaining things, she stepped over to us and told us her version of events."

"I arrived, um, a little after twelve," Darla started, "and was just about to take some photos of Mariam when the lights went out. There was, like, some screaming and stuff, and then the lights came back on. I heard Tyler say, 'That's him!' or 'Get him!' or something, and saw him pointing at the gym door, so I just turned and, like, snapped a photo."

"May I see it?" I asked.

"What do you mean?" she said.

"The picture," I said, pointing at the large camera she was holding in her hands.

"Oh, this isn't a digital camera," she said. "I develop my own photographs, Jack. You'll have to wait until tomorrow."

"You don't use a digital camera?" I asked.

"I'm an old-fashioned kind of girl," she said.

"I can appreciate that," I said. "Just let me know when it's ready."

That's when Tyler burst in on our conversation. "I don't suppose you're going to bother finding my Captain Marvel #146, Lime!"

"Just tracking down a few clues," I said.

"Chatting up chicks don't count, punchy. I thought

you'd be trying to find out which way the little snot went."

"That's a great idea, Tyler," I said. "Why don't you lead the way?"

Tyler stomped out of the gym and I followed along behind him. At that point I was feeling pretty good about my chances of solving the case. I had a room full of eyewitnesses; it'd been less than half an hour since the crime had been committed, and Darla might be able to show me a picture of the crook within twenty-four hours. The problem was I didn't know where the clues were going to lead me. If I did, I would've dropped the case faster than a burning match in a dynamite factory.

"Dropping a burning match in a dynamite factory would be a terrible idea, Jack," KC said.

"Exactly," I said.

"Sometimes you surprise me."

"I'll take that as a compliment," I said.

Wednesday, October 30, 12:44 p.m.
Iona High, The Back Lot

I asked a few people if they'd seen anyone dressed in black sprint by with a runaway comic book. They all pointed us in the direction of the rear doors. We followed the perp's trail outside and into the back lot. There were a few kids huddled under a tree, trying to stay out of the rain, and we stepped over to them.

"Yeah, sure I saw him," a tall, lanky kid said. "The dude was dressed in black and wearing a ski mask. He came out and ran into the woods over there."

I started toward the spot he was pointing at, but Tyler grabbed the poor sucker by the scruff of the neck and yanked him close.

"Why didn't you stop him?" he snapped. "Are you chicken or something?"

The kid, who was at least a foot taller than Tyler, looked around frantically for some help.

"I ... I ... I ... don't ..." the kid stammered.

"You, you, you, don't what?" Tyler said, pulling back his fist.

"Let him go, Tyler!" I yelled. "We don't have time for a shakedown. For all we know, the crook who swiped your comic is squatting in the trees right now."

Tyler looked disappointed, but he let the kid go and hustled past me into the woods.

I shrugged an apology to Tall and Lanky. He ignored me and ran back into the school. I guess he didn't want to deal with Tyler anymore. Who could blame him? I was beginning to feel the same way.

Wednesday, October 30, 12:49 p.m.
Iona High, The Back Woods

"Over here, punchy," Tyler yelled. "Quick!"

He was squatting beside a muddy trail that cut through the trees and was pointing at four fresh footprints in the mud along the path. I searched the area for any other prints, but the perp must've veered off the trail.

"That could be our man," I said, taking a close look at the nearest print. "Then again, who knows? It could belong to anyone."

"What are you saying? We give up?"

"No, Tyler," I said, "it just means we can't go jumping to any conclusions, but it would make sense for the crook to cut through here. These woods are only about fifty yards thick, and then they open up onto a street on the other side. Whoever took your comic could run through here, hightail it to the street, stash the comic somewhere, lose the ski mask and then stroll back to the front of the school like nothing happened."

"So what now?" Tyler asked.

"Let's have a look around," I said. "Maybe something will turn up."

Before we had a chance to start, the bell rang.

"It'll have to wait," I said. "I've got to get to class."

"What d'you mean?" Tyler said, stalking behind me. "We just got started!"

"What I mean is that I just wiggled my way out of a serious situation with Snit. If I step out of line, and I mean just a little, he's going to toss me out of school so fast it'll make my head spin."

"Yeah, well, we all got our problems with Snit! So what?"

"I'll tell you so what, Tyler. If I get kicked out of school, I won't be able to help you find your precious comic book, now will I?"

"Big deal. You haven't found anything anyway, punchy!" he said.

"You're wrong about that. I know the perp has feet that are about the same size as mine."

"How do you know that?"

"That footprint in the mud is about the same size as my boot," I said, pointing to my black boots. "So if those prints belong to our perp, we're looking for someone who wears size elevens, or thereabouts, and who's wearing black boots that are probably still muddy."

"How do you know they're black?"

"Everyone we've talked to said our crook was dressed in black. If the shoes were some other color, they would've stood out and someone would have mentioned it."

"That's not a lot to go on," Tyler grumbled.

"It's something to start with," I said. "So you can stay out here and look for clues all afternoon, Tyler. In fact, I hope you find your comic and we won't have to talk to each other again. But me, I'm going to class, and I'll keep my eyes peeled for someone wearing black boots, about size eleven, and muddy."

"You do that, punchy," Tyler said, "and I'll find you later."

"I hope not," I said, but he didn't hear me. He was already heading back into the woods.

Wednesday, October 30, 3:14 p.m.
Iona High, My Locker

I did a little asking around that afternoon and found out that Tyler Butt was a thug with a habit of doing some seriously bad things. He'd been kicked out of every school in the city before arriving at Iona High three weeks ago, and he'd already had a few run-ins with some of the local toughs in the Riverside Boys. Besides that, he'd managed to get on just about everyone's nerves in the school, which meant that I had a list of suspects a mile long. I was thinking I'd made a big mistake getting involved with this case when he stepped up to my locker at the end of the day.

"You see any of those black boots, punchy?" he asked.

"Afraid not," I said.

"Me neither, and I don't like the way things are shaping up," he said, poking my chest with one hard little finger.

"Did you find anything in the woods out back?"

"Nothing," he grumbled. "The footprints disappeared."

"Let me ask you something, Tyler," I said. "Do you have any idea who would want to steal that comic?"

Tyler thought for a moment. I could hear the wheels turning in his head and they sounded rusty. "Nope," he said.

"What about somebody who's into comics? Someone who knew you'd have it here today and who would want to add it to his collection? Or someone who might want to sell it?"

"Say, you're on to something there," he said, poking my chest again. "The little turd probably wants to hock it. Well, they're not going to get away with that, punchy! There's only one place in Iona that deals with used comics, and that's Pop's. You get down there and make sure nobody sells that Captain Marvel #146. You got that?"

"Sure," I said, "but what are you going to do, Tyler?"

"I'm going to take the train into the city and pay a visit to a couple of comic book shops. I want them to be real clear that if they even dream about buying my comic book off some gutless wonder, they're going to have me to deal with."

"You think that's a good idea?" I said.

"Just do what I tell you, punchy," he said. "I'll meet you at Pop's at five. Got it?"

"I got it," I said.

Based on what I'd heard about Tyler, I figured our perp would be just as likely to run that comic through a shredder for kicks and giggles as try to sell it for a pile of cabbage. But it wasn't my job to think too much. Sometimes I just had to do what my clients wanted me to do, so I headed for Pop's.

Wednesday, October 30, 4:21 p.m.
54 Main Street, Pop's Soda Bar and Comic Book Shop

Pop's Soda Bar and Comic Book Shop is owned by Luxemcorp Incorporated. The suits at Luxemcorp want us to think that some nice old man named Pop runs the place. They want us all to pretend the joint's been around since the time when you could buy a soda and a comic book for a dime and while away the hours listening to the hit parade on the jukebox. Well, I knew there wasn't anybody named Pop and I wasn't a big fan of their fake

1950s shtick, but duty called, so I shambled in and milled around in the comic book section at the back of the store. There were only four other kids flipping through the racks, and none of them were blabbing about a stolen Captain Marvel comic. After I'd spent an hour wandering around, absentmindedly scanning the comics, a portly man with a thick white mustache shuffled over.

"Do you need help finding anything, young man?"

"Just looking," I said.

"Well, son," he said, hoisting his thumb over his shoulder at a No Loitering sign, "I'm afraid you're either going to have to buy something or come back tomorrow."

Tyler would blow his stack if I left before five, so I stalled for time. "I don't suppose you've got root beer floats on the menu?"

"Vanilla or chocolate ice cream?" he asked.

"Vanilla."

"Tall or short?"

"Tall."

"Anything on the side?"

"Lemon meringue pie?"

"Coming right up," he said with a twinkle in his eye.

I took a seat in a booth close to the cash register and noticed that the walls in the dining area were covered with cartoon sketches of local citizens. Most of them I didn't know, but I spotted Principal Snit and a few of the other teachers at Iona High. I even saw one of our town's new football hero, Lance Munroe, whose giant bobble head smiled out at me from the top of a tiny body that was about to throw a football downfield, no doubt for another touchdown. I figured I'd be able to hear about any illicit transactions from there while I waited for my order and kept my eyes peeled for any suspicious activity.

Wednesday, October 30, 4:36 p.m.
54 Main Street, Pop's Soda Bar and Comic Book Shop

The old-timer with the mustache wasn't named Pop — I know because I asked (just to make sure). His name was Harry and he knew how to put together a mean root beer float. The lemon meringue pie wasn't bad either. Long story short, the food at Pop's was good enough to make me lose focus for a little while. In fact, I didn't realize I'd gotten so sloppy until Tyler slipped into the seat across from me.

"What do you got for me, punchy?"

"Huh?" I mumbled, looking up, my mouth stuffed with lemon meringue pie.

"What. Do. You. Got?" he said, his eyes bulging.

"Nothing, nada, *niet*," I said.

"One answer will do."

"How about you?" I asked. "Any luck in the city?"

"They're all a bunch of know-it-all wusses," he said. "They pretended like they couldn't care less."

"You think they know something?"

"How should I know?" he said, glancing down at my food. "What are you doing here, anyway? Just stuffing your face? You should be out there asking questions!

I thought you were supposed to be finding my Captain Marvel #146!"

"You asked me to meet you here at five o'clock. I didn't want to leave before we checked in with each other."

"You're real good at following orders, aren't you, punchy? Well, here's one for you: go find my comic book!"

"You know what," I said, sliding out of the booth and throwing my napkin on the table, "forget it! Go yell at somebody else for a while."

"You're quitting?" he said, getting out of the booth, too.

"Quitting, resigning, vacating the premises, call it whatever you like, Tyler," I said. "I'm outta here."

I started for the door, but Tyler grabbed my arm, spun me around and punched me square in the kisser. I stumbled back a few feet and got seriously miffed when I realized the coppery taste of blood was quickly replacing the wonderful taste of root beer, ice cream and lemon meringue pie that had been lingering in my mouth.

"Nobody quits on me!" he roared, and charged. This time I was ready to dodge and parry, but good ol' Harry stepped between us.

"Not in here, young buck," he said, wrapping Tyler into a bear hug and lifting him up like he was made out of feathers.

Tyler kicked and screamed, but Harry managed to haul him outside and dump him on Main Street like a sack of potatoes.

"Thanks," I said, when Harry came back in.

"Clean yourself up in the restroom and I'll get you some ice," he said. His eyes weren't twinkling anymore.

Everyone in the joint was staring at me when I came out of the little boys' room pressing a wad of paper towel to my bottom lip, which was split and swelling. Harry was standing by the front door talking to a Luxemcorp security guard.

FYI — Besides owning all the stores in town, Luxemcorp also patrols the streets using a squad of rent-o-cops who try their best to look like actual police officers. They might pass for the real thing, too, except for a red triangle-shaped patch they wear on their hearts that has Luxemcorp Inc. stitched into the middle in bold black letters.

"Here you go, kid," Harry said, handing me a white dishcloth filled with ice. "That should help with the swelling."

"Thanks," I said, taking it. The ice felt good against my lip.

"I'm Officer Reynolds," the rent-o-cop said. "I'll give you a drive home."

"I can walk," I said.

"I don't think so," Reynolds said, looking stern. "I want to have a word with your parents."

"It'll have to be my grandmother," I said.

Reynolds frowned. "You're," he started, and then flipped through a notepad he pulled out of his pocket, "Jack Lime?"

"That's right," I said, surprised he had my name jotted down in there.

"Well, I'd like to have a word with your grandmother," he said, putting the notepad away. "Just to explain what happened."

"Is that really necessary?" I said.

"I insist."

Reynolds walked me out to his cruiser, and I reached for the passenger-side door, but Reynolds opened one in the back.

"You ride in the back, kid, capiche?" he said.

"Capiche," I said, and made a mental note to take that word out of my vocabulary ASAP.

Wednesday, October 30, 5:03 p.m.
A street with no name, Grandma's House

Reynolds took me home and told my grandma that I'd spent the afternoon loitering at Pop's. He explained what happened, suggested that I find some new friends and then left in his Luxemcorp cruiser.

Grandma interrogated me about why I was hanging around at Pop's all afternoon, and I had to admit that I'd been working on a case.

"You promised you were going to stop being the town detective, Jack," she said.

"It was a momentary lapse in judgment," I admitted. "You'll be happy to know I dropped it."

She pursed her lips until they disappeared, and then grabbed the dishcloth Harry had given me. "I'll get you some fresh ice," she said. "Go put on a clean shirt for supper — yours has blood on it."

I did like she said and was coming back downstairs when she called from the kitchen to remind me to turn off the light in my bedroom. I have a bad habit of leaving it on. "I can't reach it from here, Jack," she added, and that's when I realized I'd missed a huge clue in Tyler's case.

"What did you miss?" KC asked, looking up from her notepad.

"Let me finish telling the story and you'll find out, Stone."

"Fine," she said, "but pick up the pace, Jack, I'm running out of time."

Thursday, October 31, 8:28 a.m.
Iona High, The Cafeteria

I got to school early the next morning and headed straight for the gym. The tables from Comic-Con had been put away, but I knew that Tyler's had been set up about halfway between the doors and the stage. The light switches are beside the doors, and I conducted a little experiment to see if it was possible to run from there to where Tyler's table had been and then back to the doors in under ten seconds. My best time was twelve seconds, and that didn't include turning the lights out, grabbing the right comic and weaving my way through a crowd of people in the dark.

"So somebody else had to be working the lights," KC said.

"Correctamundo, Stone! It couldn't have been a one-man job."

"But who was the accomplice?"

That's what I needed to find out, and I was hoping the photo Darla had taken just as the lights came back on would give me a clue. I headed for the cafeteria and found her sitting at a table in the corner, wearing a Batgirl costume and eating a fried egg sandwich that was dripping grease.

"What's with the costume?" I asked.

"It's Halloween, Jack."

"It must've slipped my mind," I said.

"What's with your lip?"

"It's nothing," I said, and tried to forget the fact that I'd officially taken myself off Tyler's case. "I don't suppose you developed that photo you took yesterday?"

"Sure," she said, wiping her mouth with a napkin, "but it's a little out of focus."

She pulled the photo out of her backpack and handed it over. It was big and glossy, but it wasn't in color.

"It's in black and white," I said, without taking much of a look.

"I told you, Jack, I'm an old-school kind of girl."

"Right," I mumbled, and turned my attention to the photo.

She'd been standing close to the middle of the gym when she took the photo, and it was blurry, but only a little. Through the crowd I could clearly see the culprit's left leg on the way out the door. The rest of him, or her — I'm an equal opportunity investigator — had already escaped. Whoever swiped Tyler's comic had been wearing black cargo pants with a utility pocket just above the knee and black army-style boots. I was so focused on that leg I almost didn't spot the light switches at the edge of the photo. They were by the door, and beside the light switches was an arm — a left arm poking out of a short-sleeved golf shirt. Because the picture was in black and white, I couldn't ID the color, but I'd guess it was a light shade of something, possibly yellow. Last but not least I could tell that the arm belonged to someone about my height, since the shoulder was an inch or two above the switches.

"Do you know who belongs to that arm?" I asked.

She shook her head.

"Who had the display table next to the doors?"

"Maybe you could ask somebody on Student Council," Darla said, shrugging. "They organized it."

"Mariam Singh's the president, right?"

Darla nodded, and I headed for the door.

"Jack," she called.

"Yeah?" I said, turning around.

"I need that photo back."

"What? Really? I wanted to take a closer look at it."

"We're printing the newspaper today, Jack, so I'll need the photo for the layouts. Besides, it's going to be on the front page. Everyone will have a copy by tomorrow."

Thursday, October 31, 12:06 p.m.
Iona High, The Cafeteria

I finally tracked down Mariam Singh in the cafeteria during lunch. The place was swarming with kids dressed in their finest Halloween costumes, and she was standing near the back of the room handing a card to someone dressed up as a long-haired hippie. I waited for the hippie to leave and then made my move.

"Can you guess who I am, Jack?" she asked, when I stepped up to her.

She was wearing a blue dress with a white top, blue ankle socks, ruby red shoes and carrying a picnic basket that had a small black stuffed dog hanging over the edge. Under the dog the basket was filled with black envelopes.

"The Tin Man?"

"Jack!"

"The Cowardly Lion?"

"Some detective you are," she said. "I'm Dorothy, and my little friend here is Toto," she added, giving the stuffed dog a little scratch under his stuffed chin. "Mr. Snit wouldn't let me bring a real dog."

"I've got a question for you —" I started, but she held up her hand to stop me.

"First things first, Jack. I've got a card for you. It's from a secret admirer."

She rooted around in her basket and pulled out an envelope with my name scrawled across the front in white ink.

"Trick or treat!" she said, handing over the card. "And don't forget, you could send one, too. It only costs two dollars and all the proceeds go to a good cause!"

"I'll think about it," I said, "but first I need to know who had the table next to the light switches at Comic-Con yesterday."

"Gee, I don't know," she said. "I'd have to check the Student Council records."

"Where are those?" I asked. "Can you check now?"

"Sorry, Jack," she said, smiling, "but I have to give out the rest of these cards first."

Before I had a chance to say anything else, she skipped away, leaving me there holding my silly Halloween card.

I couldn't do anything without seeing those records, so I decided to grab something to eat. While I waited in line, I ripped open the envelope she'd handed me and took out the card. A smiling jack-o'-lantern was on the front underneath the words "Trick or Treat!" On the inside, a witch was flying on a broom in front of a crescent moon. One word had been written under the witch in large red letters — "HELP!" There was a key taped to the card under that urgent message. It had an orange plastic handle with the numbers 333 printed on one side and the letters ITS on the other. Everyone in town knew that ITS stood for Iona Train Station, and the 333 would've been the number of a locker you could rent for a quarter. I tucked the key in my pocket, cut out of line and went after Mariam. She was talking to someone dressed up like Frankenstein.

"Who sent me this card?" I asked, waving it in front of her.

"I don't know, Jack," she said. "It's anonymous. And don't forget," she added, before hustling away again, "you can send one, too! It only costs two dollars and it's for a good cause!"

That key didn't have anything to do with a good cause, and a little part of me wanted to toss it in the nearest garbage can and forget about the whole thing. But I'm a PI and I wouldn't be able to look at my handsome mug in the mirror if someone landed in a heap of trouble because I ignored a cry for help. Long story short, I decided to forget about lunch and Tyler's comic for a little while. Instead I headed down to the train station to find out what was behind door number 333.

Thursday, October 31, 12:31 p.m.
The Train Station, Locker 333

I walked into the train station, stopped and cased the joint. Other than a few men and women milling around, looking at cell phones and waiting for the next train, the place was empty. I headed for the lockers, stopped ten feet in front of them and looked around again. Something wasn't right. My gut was telling me to forget about the key and hustle back to school. I scanned the room one more time, slowly, but nothing seemed out of the ordinary. Everything looked absolutely hunky-dory, completely copacetic. I figured I was just being overly paranoid, so I pulled the key out of my pocket, stepped over to locker 333 and slipped it into the lock. All my highly tuned gumshoe instincts were screaming at me to make a run for it, but I ignored them and opened the locker. There was a large manila envelope sitting inside. I pulled it out and turned it over. There was nothing written on either side. So I ripped the top open, reached inside and pulled out a comic book, a Captain Marvel #146. The next thing I knew, Tyler was snatching the comic out of my hand and Sebastian Cain was sticking a camcorder in my face.

"Caught you red-handed, Lime!" Cain exclaimed.

"No wonder you couldn't find it," Tyler barked. "You stole it!"

"Have you gone nutty, Tyler?" I said. "Why would I want to steal your comic?"

"I'll tell you why," Cain said, still aiming the camcorder at me. "To drum up business for your detective agency!"

"That's crazy!" I said.

"Is it?" Cain smirked. "You know what I think is crazy? Some loser from Los Angeles, who can't help falling asleep, pretending to be a detective. There's only one hitch, though. What happens when there are no more mysteries to solve? I'll tell you what — you start committing the crimes yourself. Then you solve them and everyone thinks you're the hero."

"You're not buying this hogwash, are you, Tyler?" I said, ignoring Cain.

"There's nothing to buy, Limey," Cain added. "I bumped into Tyler last night walking down Main Street, and he told me you dropped his case. I smelled a rat, so I offered my own investigative services. And I don't charge my clients favors. I do this for free, because there's nothing better than taking down the bad guys at Iona High, is there?"

"Nice try, Cain," I started, "but I couldn't have stolen Tyler's comic, and I have an airtight alibi to prove it."

"Oh yeah? What's your excuse?"

"I was here," I said, "on a case."

"Sure," Cain said, "and who were you working for, Santa Claus? The Tooth Fairy?"

"A kid named Jake Clam," I said. "No, wait, Jake Clum ... no, no, Jake Clim. Jake Clim, that's it."

"Are you sure that's it?" Cain said with a chuckle. "Because it kind of sounds made up to me. What do you think, Tyler?"

"Yeah," Tyler rumbled, grabbing me by the collar, "it sounds real made up."

"Plus," I added, "stealing that comic was a two-man job."

"Huh?" Tyler said.

"Listen to me, Tyler," I said, "there's no way one person could've turned out the lights, grabbed your comic and made it back to the doors in ten seconds. Somebody else had to be working the lights."

"That's not proof you didn't do it!" Cain said, lowering the camcorder.

"But it's a fact," I said to Tyler. "You solve a mystery with facts, and as soon as I find out who had the table next to the light switches in the gym, I'll be one step closer to finding out who did this to you."

"I already solved the mystery, Lime! Tyler has his comic book back. Now you're just playing mind games with us," Cain said, turning the camcorder off. "I told you he'd try to lie his way out of this."

"I'm going to smash you, Lime!" Tyler growled.

"Fine, forget about the lights for now," I said. "I wouldn't want you guys to hurt your brains thinking too hard, but I can show you Jake Clim. He'll vouch for me and that won't strain your IQ at all."

"We'll give you until the end of the day, Lime," Cain said, smirking. "You bring your little friend Jake to the front of the school by three-thirty or Tyler here is going to bust you up real good. You got that?"

"I want to bust him up right now," Tyler snarled.

"Trust me, it'll be more fun later, with a crowd watching," Cain said.

"You got till three-thirty, punchy," Tyler said, letting me go and following Cain toward the doors.

"You can thank me for finding your lousy comic some other time, Tyler!" I yelled.

Tyler stopped and turned with a crazy look in his eyes. I thought he was going to charge at me, but Cain whispered something in his ear and they both ended up laughing their way out of the train station. That was fine by me. I had other things to worry about. I needed to track down Jake Clim, and I had to do it quick, fast, in a hurry.

Thursday, October 31, 12:51 p.m.
2 Pluto Court, Iona High

I booked it back to school and ran around asking anyone and everyone if they knew a kid named Jake Clim. Nobody'd ever heard of him, and I was heading for the office to ask Van Kramp to look him up in the official database when Max Thorn stepped in front of me.

"Whoa there, Sarge, you look like a man in trouble."

"You ever heard of a kid by the name of Jake Clim? Small, blond, blue eyes."

"Negative on that, Lime," he said.

"Well, I need you to track him down, Max."

"You came to the right person for a manhunt," Max said, rubbing his hands together. "If there's a Jake Clim in this building, Sarge, I'll bring him to you, even if it means getting a little rough."

"I don't think you'll need to bother with the rough stuff, Max. He's too scrawny to put up much of a fight."

"Just the same," Max said, giving me his best salute, "I'm ready to do whatever it takes."

"If you find him, bring me the intel ASAP, got it?"

"Affirmative."

"And, Max, I need him by three-thirty or there's going to be trouble in paradise."

Max nodded and shot off down the hall while I made a beeline for the main office.

Van Kramp wasn't sitting behind his desk when I got there, so I marched down to see Snit. The door was open, and Snit and Van Kramp were standing behind his desk staring at one of two computer monitors.

"Excuse me," I said, standing in the doorway, "I'm looking for a student named Jake Clim."

"Go, Jack," Snit said, waving me out without looking away from one of the monitors. There was a low mumbling buzz coming out of it, like a hundred people all speaking at once.

"Do you know a student named Jake Clim?" I said. "I found a binder that belongs to him and I'd like to return it."

"Go, Jack!" Snit said, looking up from the monitor. "Go!"

That's when the bell rang.

"Please, I'm looking for Jake Clim. I want to return his binder. Do you know him?"

"Leave it on my desk," Van Kramp said. "I'll deal with it later."

"I'd like to give it back to him myself," I said.

"Jack," Snit said, looking back at the monitor, "I'm going to count to three. If you're not gone by the time I finish, I'm going to lock you in the suspension room for the afternoon."

"Thanks for your help," I grumbled as I walked away. I couldn't risk being locked under glass for the afternoon, not with Jake Clim out there somewhere, so I headed for class and tried to think of my next move.

Thursday, October 31, 3:31 p.m.
Iona High, My Locker

I asked every single solitary person in both my classes, including my teachers, if they knew a kid named Jake Clim. Nobody had ever heard of him. So when the final bell rang, I wandered back to my locker and got ready for my showdown with Tyler. I was just opening the door when I heard a "Psst" coming from the nearest garbage can. I shuffled over, a little nervous about what I might find, and peeked inside.

"Howdy, Sarge," Max said, staring up at me.

"What are you doing in there?"

"A little recon of my own," he said. "I do some freelance work on the side. I hope you don't mind."

"Did you manage to track down Jake Clim?"

"There's nobody at this school by that name, Sarge, and that's a Max Thorn guarantee. Did you ever consider it might be an alias?"

"Why would he use an alias?"

"I don't know," Max said. "What was the job?"

"He wanted me to record him getting hustled by a couple of brunos down at the train station, at exactly the same time that Tyler Butt's precious comic book was being stolen. And now I'm getting framed for that job and my airtight alibi has disappeared. Oh, brother," I added, as understanding dawned. "I've been such an amateur. Why didn't I see this earlier?"

"I've got a knack for clearing things up," Max said, peering over the edge of the garbage can.

"That's great, because I've got a new job for you, Max," I said. "Do you know Sebastian Cain?"

"He's a bit of an artiste, right?"

"That's the one," I said. "I need you to watch him like a hawk, stick on him like glue, become his shadow. Do you think you can manage that?"

"Affirmative," Max said, gritting his teeth. "Do you need me to take him down, too?"

"No, I don't want to spook him. I just want you to tell me where he goes and what he does for the rest of the day."

"Where and when is the rendezvous?"

"My grandma's place, tonight at ten sharp."

"Roger that, Sarge. Now I'm going to have to ask you to step away from the garbage can. You're attracting attention."

"I wouldn't want to do that," I said, and walked away. Whether I liked it or not, it was time for my meeting with Tyler Butt.

Thursday, October 31, 3:45 p.m.
Iona High, The Front Lawn

Tyler was standing in the middle of the main foyer with his arms folded across his chest when I arrived.

"Out front," he growled, and started for the doors.

"Where's Cain?" I asked, following him outside, down the steps and onto the lawn that stretched out in front of the school.

"Where's your friend?" Tyler asked, ignoring me and taking off his jacket.

"If you just give me a second to explain," I started, but Tyler wasn't in the listening mood. He just lunged at me, fists flying.

I tried to step out of the way, but he still managed to clock me in the nose. I stumbled back, a little dazed, and threw my arms up in front of my face just in time to block a barrage of blows he sent my way. Tyler stopped, stepped back and reconsidered his attack. By now a small crowd had gathered, and I took the opportunity to throw myself on top of him. I figured I had a better chance trying to smother his attack on the ground. I was wrong. I might've been four or five inches taller than Tyler, but he was as strong as an ox and as slippery as an eel. Before I knew what was happening, he had me pinned and was ready to start serving me some knuckle sandwiches. That's when somebody yanked him off me.

"That's the guy!" somebody yelled.

I sat up and saw Bucky King towering over me, holding Tyler by his shirt collar. The tall and lanky kid that Tyler had pushed around yesterday was standing a few feet away, pointing a long skinny finger at Tyler.

"That's the guy, Bucky," he said. Three toughs from the Riverside Boys were standing beside him.

"You got a problem with my friend?" Bucky asked.

"Let me go!" Tyler said. "I got work to do."

Bucky glanced in my direction and then turned back to Tyler.

"So do I," he said, and pulled back one massive fist.

I didn't stick around to see how that battle would shake down. Instead I got up and broke through the crowd. That's when Darla, still dressed as Batgirl, grabbed my arm.

"This way," she said, dragging me back up the front steps.

We'd gone through the front doors, across the main foyer and were about to head down the English wing when Snit and Van Kramp rushed outside.

"Come on," Darla said, "you need to lie low for a little while."

Thursday, October 31, 3:55 p.m.
Iona High, The Student Council Room

For those who don't know, the Student Council Room is a posh little oasis, set up next to the library, that doubles as the headquarters for the *Iona High Guardian*. It's got a few comfy sofas, some tables, its own miniature refrigerator, a microwave and a half dozen slick computers. While Darla went to grab some tissue for my bloody schnoz, I slumped down in one of the sofas and spotted an early edition of the paper. The headline across the top, in big bold black letters was one word: "STOLEN!" Underneath was Darla's black-and-white photo, but the sides had been cropped so the focus was on the perp's leg. The light switches and that mysterious left arm had been completely cut out of the action. I thought that was a bit of a travesty, since I had them figured as pretty crucial pieces of evidence, and that's when I realized that I'd missed another gigantic clue. A clue that had been literally staring back at me in black and white.

"Here," Darla said, coming back in and handing me a box of tissues. "How are you feeling?"

"Like a dope," I said, wadding two tissues up into long tubes and stuffing one up each nostril.

"Why?"

"Did you crop that photo using a computer before it went in the paper?"

"I told you, Jack," she said, "I'm an old-fashioned kind of girl. I did it manually with a cutter. To get it the way I wanted it first."

"Where?" I asked.

"At my desk, over there," she said, pointing into the corner.

"Are the clippings in here?" I asked, nodding at a garbage can sitting beside the desk.

"Probably."

I rooted through a thousand candy wrappers and potato chip bags before I found four rectangular strips that had once belonged to her large glossy photo.

I sat down and started examining each of the strips. I'd been so focused on the perp's leg and the arm beside the light switches that I hadn't really looked at the faces in the crowd.

"Bingo!" I said, waving one of the strips in the air.

"What did you find?" she asked.

"Not what, who," I said, holding the strip of photo up to her face. "That, Batgirl, is Ronny Kutcher. He's in

Grade 7 at the middle school, so there's not a reason on earth why he should be at a comic book convention at Iona High. In fact, middle school students aren't permitted in Iona High without express written permission from their principal. I know because of a case I had last year. It all had to do with a bunch of plastic bananas, a wheelbarrow and a pair of dirty underwear, but that's a story for another time."

"What now?"

"Now it's time for me to have a friendly chat with Ronny. Maybe he can explain what he was doing at Comic-Con. Heck, maybe he's even familiar with my disappearing friend Jake Clim. Thanks for the help, Darla."

I was just marching out when Mariam Singh came in.

"Oh my, Jack," she said, "what happened to your nose?"

"It's not important," I said, trying to squeeze past her.

"Are you here about the Student Council records for Comic-Con yesterday?"

"I wasn't," I said, stopping, "but what did you find out?"

"Well, according to the notes, Sebastian's table was next to the light switches."

"Sebastian Cain?"

"Uh-huh, he's one of the Grade 12 reps," Mariam said. "In fact, he planned the whole event."

I grabbed her, hugged her, kissed her on both cheeks and left. I didn't stick around for the swooning, although I'm sure she felt pretty special after all that attention from yours truly.

KC stopped with her notes and looked up. "Swooning? Really, Jack?"

Well, I was excited anyway, and I stayed that way until I got to the Kutcher place.

Thursday, October 31, 4:15 p.m.
14 Mercury Lane, The Kutcher Place

The Kutcher residence looked the same as always, a perfect slice of suburban blandness. Even at the end of October, the lawn was still perfect, the garden was still tidy and the picket fence was still very white. I strolled down the walk and knocked on the front door. I heard the pitter-patter of feet thumping toward the door and hoped they belonged to Ronny. Unfortunately, when the door opened, I found out they belonged to his older sister, Sandra.

"Jack," she said, pointing at my nose, "is that supposed to be part of your costume?"

"They're nothing," I said, pulling out the two tubes of tissue I still had rammed into my nostrils. Only now they were partially soaked with blood.

"That is so totally disgusting," she said, stepping back.

"I don't suppose you have a trash can I could throw these in?"

"No," she snapped. "Aren't you a little old to be trick or treating?"

"I'm not here about candy," I said, still holding the two bloody tissues in my hand. "I'm here to talk to Ronny. He's been a bad little boy."

"Well, he's not here, and even if he was, I wouldn't let him talk to you. Not after the way you ruined his birthday party."

"Ruined his birthday party? That's rich. I tracked down his bicycle at the bottom of the Iona River and you call that ruining his party? I was just doing my job, Sandra. A job you hired me for, by the way." I considered tossing the tissues into the garden, but I have a serious problem with littering, even on the Kutchers' property.

"Are you talking about your detective agency? That's not a job, Jack. You don't even get paid. Face it, you're a pretend detective."

"Just like you're pretending to be away at college?"

Her eyes got wide and her cheeks got red. I guess I struck a nerve.

"I'm just home for a short break," she said.

"On a Thursday?"

"It's none of your business," she spat, and started to the close the door, but I wedged my foot against it and stopped her.

"Tell Ronny I'm on to him, again," I said, and pulled my foot away.

She slammed the door and left me standing there with my two bloody tissues.

Thursday, October 31, 9:59 p.m.
A street with no name, Grandma's House

Most of the year nobody comes down our empty dead-end street, but on Halloween they can't stop. It's like a rite of passage for every elementary kid in town to wander down the lane in the dark and knock on our front door. There are rumors that my grandmother's a witch, and all those scared little saps are usually about ready to leap out of their costumes by the time they ring our doorbell. I spent the evening sitting on the front porch, giving out handfuls of candy to frightened kids and waiting for Max to show up.

I was expecting him to burst out of the darkness with his face painted green and wearing army fatigues. Instead he strolled up the front walk dressed like a circus clown, carrying a pillowcase half filled with candy.

"Hello, Sarge," he said, stepping onto the porch.

"What's with the getup, Max?"

"It's Halloween, Lime. I needed to blend in. You didn't expect me to march around dressed in my army fatigues, did you?"

"Of course not," I said. "So, Captain Clown, what did you find out?"

"I tracked Cain to his house, where he had dinner with his family. They had spaghetti and meatballs with garlic bread. He had seconds. After dinner he put on a black hooded cloak and a white featureless mask. Then he grabbed a backpack and left the premises by himself. This was at 7:02 p.m. I followed him to Main Street, and he entered Pop's Soda Bar and Comic Book Shop at precisely 7:27 p.m. According to the sign on the door, Pop's was hosting a Luxemcorp Incorporated Halloween Party. Unfortunately it was only open to employees of Luxemcorp and their children."

"How do you know?" I asked.

"A security guard stopped me at the door and asked for my invitation. Thankfully my dad hasn't sold out to the bums at Luxemcorp, not yet anyway, so I had to turn around and watch the action from across the street. Luckily I brought these," he said, pulling a pair of miniature binoculars out of his pillowcase.

"Dressed like a clown?"

"Like I said, Lime, I didn't want to attract attention."

"Right."

"At the party Cain met with another individual who was also wearing a black cloak and the same featureless mask. Cain removed a small camcorder from his backpack and handed it to this individual, who took it and left immediately."

"Did you follow him? Did you get a look at his face? Was he short?"

"He was on the short side, Sarge, but I didn't get a look at his face. And, no, I didn't follow him," he said. "My orders were to follow Cain."

"I don't think you're going to get that promotion you were looking for, Thorn," I said.

"My orders were to follow Cain," he said, standing at attention.

"Fine, fine, go on."

"Cain then met with two other individuals."

"Who?"

"Mike Anderson, aka Mike the Bookie, and Ronny Kutcher. They sat at a booth together for about twenty minutes, had a few laughs and then Cain left and went back home for the rest of the evening."

"Okay. All right," I said, nodding.

"What's our next move, Sarge?"

"Stand down," I said. "I'll take it from here."

"You can't yank me off a mission that easily, Lime. I'll stand back, but I'll be watching," he said, pointing at his eyes. "I'll be watching," he repeated, and then he ran to the end of the porch and dove over the railing. I heard him crash on the other side. By the sound of his screams, I was guessing he landed in one of Grandma's thorn-infested rosebushes.

"Are you okay, Max?" I called.

"Fine," he croaked, limping around the corner of the house. "I'll be watching," he repeated, and then he slowly disappeared into the darkness.

Friday, November 1, 8:14 a.m.
2 Pluto Court, Iona High

I was formulating a complicated sting that I was hoping would help me take down Cain and his crew when I walked into school the next day and ran into a giant galoot from the football team named Jerry Pyle. Jerry was three times my size and knocked me on the floor.

"You should watch where you're going, Lime," he said, standing over me.

"I got caught thinking about something, Jerry," I said, standing up and dusting myself off. I'd done a job for Jerry's little brother last spring. It was an open-and-shut case, but Jerry had been pleased as punch that I'd helped him out. So I was a little surprised to see him looking down at me like he was about to squish a bug.

"Well, maybe you shouldn't do so much thinking," Jerry said.

"Huh?" I said.

"And you can forget about collecting that favor Tommy owes you, big guy. You stay away from him if you know what's good for you. You got it?"

"Sure," I mumbled, as Jerry stalked off.

I turned, took about a dozen steps and got shoved into the lockers.

"You think you're real clever, don't you, Lime?" This time a cat named Billy Stevens was sticking his nose in my face. "You think we're all a bunch of chumps, don't you? Well, why don't you take your crime show back to LA where it belongs."

"What are you talking about, Billy?" I said, pushing him away from me.

But it wasn't just Billy giving me the squeeze — there were five or six other mooyuks crowding in behind him, and they all looked mad as heck.

He pushed me back against the lockers, and my head snapped against the metal hard enough to make my eyes go buggy. "What, are you going to pretend to fall asleep now?"

"Back off," I said, and gave him a hard shove this time, but his friends caught him and they all started pressing in on me again.

It was looking pretty grim when Lance Munroe burst through the crowd with his fists up. "You're going to have to go through me first!" he said. Lance might be a pretty boy, but being the school's star quarterback commands respect, so Billy and his friends started to back off.

"You're lucky your boyfriend's here," Billy said. "But he can't watch your back 24/7. We'll be seeing you soon, Lime."

Lance grabbed my shoulder and dragged me into an empty hallway.

"What's going on?" I asked. "Has everyone gone loony?"

"It's the video, Jack," he said.

"What video?"

"Somebody posted a video of you online and made it look like you stole Tyler Butt's comic book."

"That's Sebastian Cain or one of his cronies," I said. "And people actually believe that hoo-ha?"

"Well, it is online," he said, "and it gets worse, too, Jack. They kind of made it seem like you've been behind all the crimes at Iona High. Like you've been committing them so you can solve them, and then you end up looking like a big hero."

"What a bunch of baloney," I grumbled.

"I know it's baloney. I know what you did for me, Jack, and I'm pretty sure you weren't behind any of those other crimes, but a lot of people think it's true. I think you should go home and lie low for a couple of days, maybe a whole week. At least until things get straightened out."

"What, so people can drag my good name through the mud? I don't think so, bub."

"I'm only trying to help you, Jack."

"Listen to me, Lance, I'm real close to cleaning up this mess, and when I do, people will know the truth. Plus, things can't get any worse."

"I don't know, Jack, I think things could get worse, probably a lot worse."

And then, right on cue, Mr. Snit's voice came over the PA. "Would Jack Lime please report to the office. That's Jack Lime, to the office. Immediately."

"Say hello to Betty for me," I said, and turned around.

"Go home, Jack," Lance called as I walked away. "Go home until all this blows over!"

I'd be darned if I was going to run away now. This was just Cain playing his dirty version of hardball. Well, I could handle dirty. I could handle dirty just fine.

Friday, November 1, 8:24 a.m.
Iona High, Snit's Office

"Close the door, Jack," Snit said when I walked into his office, "and sit down. I want to talk to you about something I saw yesterday."

"The video's a hoax," I said, sitting down. "I didn't do it."

"What are you talking about, Jack? I know you were involved. I saw it with my own two eyes."

"Yeah, well," I said, "sometimes your eyes can play tricks on you."

"Look at this," he said, swiveling one of two monitors he had on his desk toward me, "and tell me if my eyes are playing tricks on me."

I was expecting to see an amateur-looking conspiracy video made by Cain and his merry band of fiendish friends. Instead I was looking at Tyler Butt and me facing off on the school's front lawn. We were frozen in time for a second, and then Snit must've pressed Play because I heard myself say, "If you just give me a second to explain." That's when Tyler sprang at me like a hungry tiger at a sheep farm. I watched myself try to step out of the way, but not quickly enough, and I couldn't help gingerly touching my nose when Tyler hit me in the video. Then I was blocking Butt's punches, and doing a pretty good job of it, when Snit pressed Pause.

"Are my eyes playing tricks on me, Jack?" he asked.

"How did you record that?" I asked. "There are no security cameras here."

"As you know, this school is owned and operated by Luxemcorp Incorporated, and they've been eager to install security cameras since this fine facility was built. However, as the principal, I felt that the cameras would invade the students' privacy, and I've fought tooth and nail to keep them out of Iona High. Unfortunately, since Tyler Butt's comic book was stolen, the folks at Luxemcorp have decided to install eight top-of-the-line security cameras at our school. They're very eager to stop any future crimes."

"Really," I said.

"Yes, and they'll be rolling twenty-four hours a day, seven days a week. I called you down to make sure that you're okay and to let you know that we are aware of the incident that occurred with Tyler Butt and are taking the necessary steps to make sure it doesn't happen again."

"What do you mean, 'the necessary steps'?"

"Well, unfortunately it means that Mr. Butt has been permanently expelled from Iona High. So you can rest assured that he won't be bothering you on school grounds again."

"Wow, that makes me feel so much safer," I said. "What about Bucky King?"

"I can't comment on that, Jack, but I wanted to show you this video so you know, once and for all, that you can take a break from trying to police this school. Obviously we can handle that just fine without you. You can go back to focusing on your schoolwork. And, Jack, for the record, these cameras are supposed to be a secret. None of the students, including you, are supposed to know that they've been installed. Do you understand what I'm saying?"

"I understand," I said. "I'll keep it on the q.t."

"Before you go, are you sure you're all right?"

"I'm fine, Mr. Snit," I said, standing up. "By the way, have they installed cameras at the middle school, too?"

"And the elementary," he said.

"And they all have audio?"

"Only the finest for Luxemcorp. You can sleep easy, Jack — we'll be one step ahead of the bad guys now."

"I think you might be right, Mr. Snit," I said. "I think you might be right."

Friday, November 1, 12:45 p.m.
21 Titan Trail, Iona Middle School

I only got accosted about a half dozen times that morning by angry clods who had watched Cain's video and bought his outrageous lies hook, line and sinker. But that didn't faze me. I had bigger fish to fry and a plan that needed to be put into action. So at lunch I strolled over to Iona Middle School. The way I figured it, Ronny Kutcher was the weak link in all of this, and I wanted to see what I could wring out of him.

I arrived there about halfway through the lunch break and got comfortable under a big tree across the street. Ronny lived close enough to the school to go home for lunch, so I played the odds and waited to catch him coming back. He arrived about fifteen minutes before the bell rang, riding a red mountain bike. He pulled up to the fence on the side of the parking lot and locked it up. While he was doing that, I made a beeline for the front doors and scanned the walls for a hidden camera. I had to hand it to the suits at Luxemcorp — obviously they didn't mind spending a few bucks on their surveillance equipment, and I was betting someone in the head office was excited about this cloak-and-dagger stuff. The tiny camera was encased in the wall just above the front door, between two bricks, and if Snit hadn't told me they'd been installed, I never would've spotted it. By now Ronny was strolling toward the side of the school, whistling "Happy Birthday" and looking smug.

"Hello, Ronny," I called, "fancy meeting you here."

He stopped whistling and frowned. "What are you doing here, Lime?"

"I'm here to give you a last chance."

"What's that supposed to mean?" he said, coming over to meet me.

"I've got a photo of you in the gym at Iona High about five seconds after Tyler Butts's comic was stolen."

"So what?" he said, his little eyes shifting from the left to the right.

"I'll tell you so what, buster. That photo places you at the scene of the crime, and I'm willing to bet that I can find a few witnesses who would ID you as the sap that tripped up Tyler when he tried to go after the perp."

"There's no law against tripping someone," he said.

"No," I said, inching backward, a little closer to the camera, "but I'm sure you're aware there is a rule against middle school students loitering at Iona High."

"I just wanted to see the comics."

"Well, that's just the thing, Ronny. I'm going to have to show that photo to Mr. Snit and then he's going to have to show it to your principal and then they're going to start asking you questions. And I'm betting that a tyke like you won't hold up all that well when you're sitting in an office, feeling the squeeze from your principal. Especially when I throw in a few eyewitnesses who will confirm you were aiding and abetting a criminal like Sebastian Cain."

Ronny's mouth dropped open.

"Oh sure, I know Cain had the table next to the doors and was working the lights for this insidious operation. It's only a matter of time before I can prove that Mike the Bookie was the one who snatched Tyler's comic."

"What ... how ... no ..."

"Quit with the mumbling, Ron. It doesn't suit someone of your diminutive stature. You shouldn't've met with each other last night at Pop's, not so soon after the crime. Plus, Mike's my height and build. You cover him up in black and nobody would know the difference."

"That doesn't prove anything," he said.

"Maybe, maybe not, but when I pull out that photo, the ball's going to start rolling and it's heading right at you, Ronny. One way or another, you're getting squished, and that's why I'm your last chance. You might be able to toss a bicycle in a river, but you're not smart enough, or bold enough, to pull off a sting like this. So who's the wizard behind the curtain? Is it Cain? Is it Mike?"

He giggled.

"Something funny?"

"You're wrong again, Lime," he said, grinning up at me.

"Who's in charge, Ronny? Fess up or you're going down."

He giggled some more. I wanted to grab him and shake him a bit, but I'd lured him closer to that hidden camera for a reason and I couldn't risk losing my cool.

"Spit it out, kid! I know it wasn't you! You're just a pint-sized pip-squeak that they used to trip up Tyler. So stop your snickering and spit it out!"

Ronny quit with the chuckling quick, fast, in a hurry. "You're wrong! It wasn't Mike or Cain or Bucky!" he said. "It was me, me and my friend. We planned it, we stole the comic and we pinned it on you, Limey. Mike and Cain were just following orders. They just did whatever ... my friend told them to do."

"What friend?" I said.

He smiled. "My friend is smart, Jack. Smarter than you. My friend knows about a lot of different things and is going to beat you and make you leave Iona forever."

"I don't have time for your kind of crazy, Ronny," I said. "I guess I'm going to have to show Mr. Snit that photo, after all. Good luck with your nutty tale when you're getting the squeeze from the powers that be."

I pushed past Ronny and was starting down the stairs when an extremely tall black-haired lady wearing a navy blue suit came striding across the parking lot.

"Excuse me!" she called, barreling toward me. "What are you doing here?"

"He said he was going to beat me up!" Ronny cried, before I even had a chance to open my mouth.

"He was threatening me! He wanted money, Mrs. Snurt!" Ronny continued, blathering behind me.

"Who are you, young man?" she asked.

"Who are you?" I asked.

"I'm the principal here," she said, glaring at me. "Now answer the question, who are you?"

"I'm Jack Lime."

"*The* Jack Lime?" she said, her eyebrows shooting up.

"That's right."

"Well, I think we all need to step inside," she said, practically sprinting up the stairs and opening the door. "Now!"

"My pleasure," I said.

"He said he wanted twenty dollars or he'd beat me up," Ronny said, rushing past me.

"Don't worry, I'll get to the bottom of this," Snurt said, marching down the hallway.

She hustled down to the main office, told us to take a seat and turned to a blond woman who was sitting behind the desk, furiously typing away on a laptop.

"May I have a word with you, Ms. Van Kramp?" Snurt asked.

"Ms. Van Kramp?" I blurted.

"Yes, I'm Elizabeth Van Kramp," she said, looking over at me. She had dazzling blue eyes, the color of the sky on a perfect summer day, and was wearing a red skirt with a red sleeveless top and a strand of pearls around her neck. She was a knockout, and if I hadn't been in the middle of a case, I might've asked her out for a root beer float, despite the small age difference. I also noticed she had a British accent that matched Mr. Van Kramp's. "May I help you?"

"Are you married to Mr. Van Kramp?" I asked.

"He's my older brother," she said, flashing me a flawless smile.

"Ms. Van Kramp," Snurt said again, "just a moment of your time, please."

They stepped into a far corner of the room, and Snurt started explaining the situation in a whisper. I was about to give Ronny one more chance to come clean when I noticed three photos taped to the wall beside the door. Each belonged to a different kid, and under each one was an allergy warning. Normally that kind of thing wouldn't give me a small heart attack, except the photo on the far right belonged to a kid that I recognized. It was a small boy with blond hair and blue eyes. I knew him as Jake Clim, but the name under his photo said Tomas Van Kramp.

"Tomas Van Kramp!" I exclaimed, leaping out of my chair. "Tomas Van Kramp!"

"What?" Ms. Van Kramp said, turning to me.

"Tomas Van Kramp," I said, turning to Ronny. "He planned it all, didn't he?"

Ronny just stared straight ahead.

"What?" Ms. Van Kramp asked.

"Is he your son?" I asked.

"No," she said, frowning. She looked downright insulted and I think our future together was in serious jeopardy. "He's my younger brother. What did you say about him?"

"Oh, nothing," I said, sitting back down, "but I think Ronny is his friend. He's your friend, isn't he, Ronny? He's your very smart friend, isn't he?"

"Stop picking on me!" Ronny wailed.

Snurt stalked across the room. "Now see here," she said, "high school students are not permitted on the middle school grounds, and they're certainly not allowed to intimidate my students."

"You can't prove anything," I said, waving her away. "It's his word against mine."

Snurt's eyes blazed. "Come with me," she said through clenched teeth. "You stay here, Ronny," she added, and led me down to her office.

"Take a seat," she said, closing the door behind us.

I did as she asked and noticed that she had two monitors on her desk, just like Snit. This whole crazy gambit might actually pay off.

"You can't prove anything," I said again.

She pursed her lips, sat down at her desk and fumbled around with a few buttons on her computer.

We sat there in silence for about thirty seconds, and then she looked up and glared at me. "Now we'll see," she said, swiveling the monitor around so that I could see the screen, "who's telling the truth."

There I was, the star of the show, in Technicolor, standing in front of the school, frozen in time.

"You didn't expect this, did you, Mr. Lime?" she said. Before I could answer, she pressed Play.

"Hello, Ronny," I said, "fancy meeting you here."

We sat there and watched the whole give-and-take between me and Ronny play out. I have to admit, I enjoyed watching Snurt's face go from confident to confused when Ronny started chirping about how he and his friend had stolen Tyler's comic. By the time she came striding onto the screen to confront me, her face had gone from confused to just old-fashioned angry.

"High school students are not permitted on the middle school grounds. I don't want to see you here again," she said, stopping the video clip and standing up. "Now if you'll excuse me, I'd like to have a word with Ronny."

"I have more proof," I said. "I've got a photo of Ronny in the gym, moments before Tyler Butts's comic was stolen. Plus, if you ask to see the security tapes at the train station, they'll corroborate my alibi and prove that Tomas Van Kramp met with me there two days ago. They might also show who actually put Tyler's comic book in the locker. And that's the truth, Ms. Snurt."

"Thank you, Mr. Lime. I'll be contacting Mr. Snit this afternoon. We'll investigate this matter together," she said. "Could you please tell Ronny to see me on your way out."

"My pleasure," I said, and left.

When I strolled into the main office, I told Ronny that Snurt wanted to have a little chat. Ronny got white in the face and weak in the knees. I think I even heard his teeth chattering as he walked by.

"Say hello to Tomas for me," I said to Ms. Van Kramp on my way out.

"Does he know you?" she asked, looking up from her laptop.

"We met once," I said and headed back to school.

Friday, November 1, 4:59 p.m.
A street with no name, Grandma's House

"That all went down today at lunch," I said, looking across the kitchen table at KC. "By two o'clock I was getting hauled down to Snit's office for an emergency meeting. I got the impression that Ronny cracked faster than an egg in an omelet shop and spilled the beans about everything. Snit even asked me about Tomas Van Kramp and our meeting at the train station. On my way out, I got to say a friendly hello to Cain and Mike the Bookie, who were sitting in the main office looking glum. Long story short, their criminal organization is getting blown apart like a deck of cards in a hurricane. Just the same, half the school still thinks I'm a two-bit scam artist, thanks to that video, so I'm sure you can see how having this story in your newspaper would help clear my name."

"I can see that, Jack," she said, "but I don't know if I can run it."

"What do you mean, you don't know if you can run it? This is the biggest crime story to ever come out of Iona High."

"I don't know if Mr. Snit would let me print it if Tomas Van Kramp is involved."

"What's so important about Tomas Van Kramp?"

"You know who the Van Kramps are, right, Jack?"

"A family with a knack for producing school secretaries?"

"They're not actually the secretaries, Jack."

"What are you talking about?"

"Do you know who Anton Van Kramp is?"

"Should I?"

"Anton Van Kramp owns Luxemcorp, Jack. Born in Switzerland, sixty-four years old, and the seventh richest man in the world. He's currently married to Maria Van

Kramp, and they have three children: Victor, Elizabeth and Tomas."

"You know a lot about Anton Van Kramp," I said.

"It's my job to know things, Jack. Basically the Van Kramps own this town."

"Well, what are they doing traipsing around like they're secretaries?"

"Anton Van Kramp has built towns like Iona all over the world, and he's a real stickler for details. So he travels around with his family checking up on things. Mr. Snit isn't Mr. Van Kramp's boss — it's the other way around."

"So you're afraid to print the story even though these yahoos tried to frame me for a crime I didn't commit?"

"I don't think Mr. Snit will run it."

"Then run it yourself, KC. This is the scoop of a lifetime."

"My parents work for Luxemcorp, Jack," she said, looking down at her notepad. "If I wrote a story that said Tomas Van Kramp was a criminal mastermind, without a mountain of evidence, they might get in trouble, and I don't want to risk that."

"Evidence?" I said. "Jake Clim is Tomas Van Kramp. I saw him with my own two eyes, Stone. And once Snit checks the security cameras at the train station, he'll see that Tomas met me there, just like I said! There's some evidence for you."

"I'm sorry, Jack," she said, collecting her things, "but I can't run the story, not until I get a few more facts."

"Fine," I said, banging the table and getting up, too, "but you can forget about any more interviews."

"I'm sorry to hear that," she said.

"I'm not," I said, escorting her out of the kitchen, through the living room and over to the front door. "So long, KC," I said, holding the door open.

"Thanks for the pumpkin pie," she called to my grandma. "It was delicious."

"You're welcome, dear," Grandma said.

"The next time you hear about a damsel in distress, Stone, go ask someone else for help. I'm closed for business."

She nodded, stepped outside, and I slammed the door.

I was halfway up the stairs and heading for my room when the phone rang.

"It's for you, Jack," Grandma called from the kitchen.

I went back downstairs and took the phone.

"Hello."

"Hello, Jack," a robotic voice said on the other end. I glanced down at the call minder. The number was 555-3333.

"Who is this?"

"You've ruined everything, you know. My whole team is going up in flames. Do you have any idea how difficult it is to infiltrate the Riverside Boys? Do you know how much work that is?"

"Tomas?" I said.

The caller laughed. "Jake Clim? Does anybody know a Jake Clim? Jeesh, Jack, sometimes you make me wonder."

"Mike?"

"Believe me, Jack, Mike isn't smart enough to run something like this. He couldn't even hang on to his little black book, for Pete's sake. No, Mike and Cain, Ronny and Tomas — they all needed to be steered in the right direction. They needed leadership, Jack."

"And you're their rotten leader, is that it?"

"First I go through all the trouble of getting Lance under my thumb, and you ruin it. Me and my associates could have made a lot of money off of Lance, and the cavemen in the Riverside Boys would've thanked us. I didn't think you could save him, or I never would've sent Betty your way. I thought you would just show the world what a fool you really are, and maybe get expelled along the way, but oh no, you managed to bumble through it somehow."

"Bumble through it?" I said. "Let me tell you something, I —"

"Stop! Just stop talking! I'm tired of listening to you talk! I've been listening to you talk for too long. I'm trying to vent here, Jack, and you're interrupting my villainous monologue."

"You like big words, don't you?" I said.

"I'm sorry, are those words too big for you, Jack? How's this — you're cutting me off! I'm trying to explain things to you and you don't have the brains to shut up and listen."

"I'm shutting up," I said.

"Good. First you ruin everything with Lance, then we frame you for stealing Mike's 'diary' and you wiggle out of that, too. So, then I have to go and spend all my free time getting close to Anton Van Kramp and his little cretin of a son, Tomas. I was lucky that my parents work for Luxemcorp, and it helped that I could tell him I was on official school business, otherwise he never would've let me through the door. I had to do a lot of research for him to buy that one. It's not easy getting close to the Van Kramps, but with a Van Kramp on your side, you can get things done."

"Criminal things."

"Oh, Jack, what's a crime to you is just plain fun for me. It's all in the eye of the beholder, don't you think?"

"A crime is a crime, no matter what way you try to cut it."

"Getting rid of a bully like Tyler Butt is a crime? I don't think so."

"You tried to frame me!" I said.

"Yes we did, and all my planning would've paid off if Ronny could've kept his tiny mouth shut. Do you have any idea how annoying it is to watch an imbecile like you stumbling around, solving crimes through sheer luck, while someone like me spends so much time and effort planning perfect schemes? I couldn't laugh you off anymore, Lime. I simply had to get rid of you."

"Looks like you failed, compadre."

"I don't think so. The video's still out there, and that's what people are going to believe. The damage is done. You're through in this town."

"This is getting old, and fast. Turn off that robot voice and tell me who you are. Then we can finish this mano a mano. Or are you too yellow?"

"You're right, Jack, this is getting old. I guess you're not the only one who likes to hear themselves talk. As for the yellow part, I'm not afraid of you, I just thought a detective of your stature would have more serious problems to deal with — like hangnails and out-of-control nose hairs."

Hang nails and out-of-control nose hairs? Who'd said that to me? Someone who got close to the Van Kramps. Someone who had parents that work for Luxemcorp. Someone who could say they were on official school business. Someone who'd been listening to me talk for a long time. Someone who sent Betty my way.

"KC?" I said, but the line was dead, and then my condition kicked in, and I fell into a deep dark hole called sleep.

THE END

The names of the people and places haven't been changed to protect the innocent. Everything is exactly as it happened.